# DaVinci's
# CAT

CATHERINE GILBERT MURDOCK

# DaVinci's CAT

**A
Novel**

DECORATIONS BY
Paul O. Zelinsky

GREENWILLOW BOOKS
*An Imprint of* HarperCollins*Publishers*

Many thanks to historian Brad Bouley for his excellent insights
into Renaissance Rome, disease, wages, and schoolwork.
—C. G. M.

Da Vinci's Cat
Copyright © 2021 by Catherine Gilbert Murdock
Illustrations copyright © 2021 by Paul O. Zelinsky

All rights reserved. No part of this book may be used or reproduced in any manner whatsoever without
written permission except in the case of brief quotations embodied in critical articles and reviews. Printed
in the United States of America. For information address HarperCollins Children's Books, a division of
HarperCollins Publishers, 195 Broadway, New York, NY 10007.
www.harpercollinschildrens.com

The text of this book is set in 13-point Nicolas Jenson SG.
Book design by Paul Zakris

Library of Congress Cataloging-in-Publication Data

Names: Murdock, Catherine Gilbert, author.
Title: Da Vinci's cat / a novel by Catherine Gilbert Murdock.
Description: First edition. | New York : Greenwillow Books, an imprint of HarperCollins Publishers, 2021. |
Audience: Ages 8-12. | Audience: Grades 4-6. |
Summary: Using a mysterious wardrobe that allows them to travel through time, two eleven-year-olds,
Federico a boy from the Italian Renaissance and Bee a girl from present-day New Jersey, work together
to prevent the bickering between two great artists from changing the future.
Identifiers: LCCN 2020053868 | ISBN 9780063015258 (hardcover) |
ISBN 9780063015272 (ebook)
Subjects: CYAC: Time travel—Fiction. | Michelangelo Buonarroti, 1475-1564—Fiction. |
Raphael, 1483-1520—Fiction.
Classification: LCC PZ7.M9416 Dad 2021 | DDC [Fic]—dc23
LC record available at https://lccn.loc.gov/2020053868
21 22 23 24 25 PC/LSCH 10 9 8 7 6 5 4 3 2 1
First Edition

Greenwillow Books

To Virginia

# Contents

## Part I: Then

## Part II: Now, and Then

## Part III: Plans Fail

## Part IV: The Untangling

# PART I

# THEN

## Chapter 1
## THE VISITOR

Federico leaped to his feet, reaching for his knife though he was still half asleep. "Papa!" he shouted. "Alarms!" A face loomed at him out of the darkness. But Federico had no knife at his waist—not even a belt—

Oh. Oh. He exhaled, lowering his arms in relief. That face was not an enemy but only an antique statue, a gift from his mother. She lived far to the north with Papa and Federico's sisters, in a castle with five hundred rooms. Federico, however, had dwelled this past year in Rome, in a villa that served as his prison.

Again alarms blared—no, not alarms but trumpets, announcing the next course of a banquet. Laughter drifted through the window, and the scents of mustard sauce, mutton, onions, spicy oysters, fish roasted with citrus. . . . Musicians tootled and twanged. Between the slats of the shutter, Federico could see a courtyard graced with tall marble sculptures and slim cypress trees, and a table crowded with diners. Even now a jester back-flipped along the tabletop, flicking the candles with his toes.

Federico himself should be out there with the other guests, hooting at the jester's antics. But this afternoon he'd gone to bed with a headache. Now the trumpets had startled him awake, his headache replaced by irritation and no small amount of hunger.

He could, he supposed, slink down and join the meal. But a gentleman did not slink. A gentleman made an entrance at the proper moment, to the approval of the crowd. To show up like a fretful child after a nap? Besides, he wasn't a child. He had eleven years. He was almost a man.

Glumly Federico studied the scene: the flickering candelabras, the glint of crystal and silver, the bowls of perfumed water and floating petals. Gems twinkled on the guests' fingers, on their caps, in their hair. Once more the trumpets sounded as footmen carried in a platter with a roasted boar's head coated in gold.

The sight of the boar doubled Federico's hunger—the

cherry sauce smelled so good! He must eat. But what? Not his elegant silk bedspread, or the portrait of his father in shining black armor, or his schoolbooks and pens and ink . . . The travel chest might contain something. It was nearly the size of a coffin, meant to hold all the items needed for a long stay such as his.

Federico dug through the layers, careful not to snag his rings. There: a pot of sugared almonds. They only took the edge off his appetite. He frowned as he swabbed out the last of the sugar. At home, he could sneak to the kitchens for candied lemons or spiced bonbons in syrup. But no chef in Rome would make the effort to preserve such luxuries for him.

Federico sighed, belly rumbling. He wanted something sweet! Fruit, even. Grapes, or figs—

Figs. But of course. This very morning he'd seen a platter of figs in the pope's new study. Federico had been sitting for hours as Master Raphael Sanzio painted his portrait onto the wall, and the figs were a nice interruption. He and Raphael had eaten several and left the rest on a windowsill.

Again Federico's belly growled, for a moment drowning out the snores of his governess in the next room. But the figs were all the way in the pope's palace. Should he wander so late without servants or guards—without even waking Celeste?

His stomach grumbled an answer: yes.

Quickly Federico pulled on silk breeches and hose. They did not match but no one would see him. He strapped on a knife belt and tied a cloak round his shoulders, for a gentleman without a cloak might as well be naked. Setting a cap on his blond curls, he took up the lantern that Celeste kept burning *just in case* and tiptoed out the door. Federico might be a hostage, kept in Rome to guarantee his family's loyalty to His Holiness, Pope Julius II. But that did not mean he was trapped in his room.

The villa in which Federico resided sat on a high breezy hill, almost a quarter mile from the pope's palace. His Holiness had recently decided to link the two buildings with a long corridor in order to impress his guests. This corridor was still very much under construction, however, and few but Federico used it. Workmen stored planking there, and unwanted furniture. At this hour the moon gaped through the half-built roof. Federico's lantern made eerie shadows out of ladders and stacks of tiles and a man hulking by the wall—

Federico jumped back, heart pounding. It wasn't a man! Just a large wooden box. Thank heavens his sisters weren't here, for they would have been frightened. But not him.

Still, he averted his eyes as he crept past the box.

At last he reached the end of the corridor and the heavy door to the palace. The pope's palace, too, was under construction, every room and hallway requiring some new decoration or shape. Federico had to sidestep boxes of tools and tubs of quicklime as he made his way to the pope's new study. He reached for the door—and sniffed. Unwashed feet, dirty clothes, greasy hair . . . He knew those smells. "Master?" he called, wrinkling his nose. "Michelangelo?"

The study door burst open. "Who is it?" Michelangelo glared down, fists clenched. "Hmph. Federico. What do you want?"

What a strange creature Michelangelo Buonarroti was. The greatest sculptor in the world, more talented than even the Ancients—but his pride drove away admirers and his misery drove away friends. Years of looking up to paint the Sistine Chapel ceiling had left his neck permanently crooked. Long ago he'd had his nose broken for bragging, and his father had warned him never to bathe. Michelangelo wasn't handsome to begin with, but with his mangled face and his stink . . .

"Good evening, Master." Federico bowed, breathing through his mouth. Why was Michelangelo here? "I've come to . . . admire my portrait." That sounded more respectable than admitting to hunger—hunger was what poor people felt. He slipped past Michelangelo into the study. Sheets covered the bookcases and the floor; rough platforms allowed painters to reach upper walls. There, on the windowsill: the platter. "Ah. Figs." He held the platter out. "Would you like some?"

Michelangelo waved the fruit away. "Your portrait?" he scoffed. "Portraits aren't art."

"Sometimes they are." Federico's eyes went to a handsome blond boy above the door—one small painted figure tucked into a scene of fifty-odd philosophers. *Such a joy it is to include you,* Raphael had said as he applied the finishing touches. *You look wise beyond your years.*

Michelangelo glared at the crowded wall. "Everything that peacock knows, I taught him." Peacock was Michelangelo's name for Raphael, to mock Raphael's fine clothes.

Federico almost choked on a fig. "I didn't know Master Raphael was your student."

"I didn't say he was my student. I'd never allow such a thing. He simply takes. Like a hole in a bucket draining me empty. Like a leech sucking out blood."

"Ah." Federico lowered the platter. Now he felt queasy.

Michelangelo scowled at an image of philosopher Pythagorus

displaying his theory of harmony. "What do you and Raphael talk about? Do you two talk about me?" Though only six and thirty, the artist's face held lines of misery. He reeked of sweat and old boots.

Federico risked another fig. "Mostly we talk about His Holiness. Raphael likes to hear about him throwing the backgammon table." Federico played backgammon with the pope, and often won.

"The peacock is desperate to see the Sistine Chapel, you know. But I'll never allow it." Michelangelo glowered at the wall, the figures so perfect that they were almost breathing. "Hmph." Away he stomped, trailing stink.

Well. That was interesting, Federico thought as he headed back to the villa. What was Michelangelo doing in the pope's study in the middle of the night? The palace decorations were Raphael's assignment, nothing to do with him. Federico gasped as the truth hit him: Michelangelo had been spying! The great master, secretly studying young Raphael. What a delicious bit of gossip.

But whom could Federico tell? Celeste talked so much that she had no time to listen. The few children in the palace worked as pages or cook's boys, far below his rank; a

duke's son did not socialize with commoners. The footmen—
his tailor—the jester? The cupids painted on his ceiling? No.
Though Federico knew many souls in Rome, he had no one
to call a friend.

He pondered this sad truth, gloomily chewing the last fig,
as he trekked down the corridor. Somewhere in the distance
the church of Saint Mary Major rang midnight, the mournful
sound matching his mood. Gravel scratched beneath his slippers; his lantern barely dented the black. The stars watched
him coldly. How he wished for the company of his little sisters. How he wished to be home. Not for the first time, he
thought about running away. Such a crime, however, would
bring his whole family shame. No, he must remain captive in
Rome until His Holiness saw fit to release him—

"Mrow."

What was that? Federico spun, drawing his knife. Pearly
moonbeams pierced the darkness, lighting pyramids of floor
tile and stacks of planks and the tall wooden box by the
wall. . . . He frowned. What was that box doing here,
anyway? It must have arrived this afternoon, during his nap.

Screwing up his courage, Federico eased closer, knife in
hand. The box—some kind of closet—was a fine piece, to be

sure, with gems set into smooth walnut wood. Someone had paid well for the carpentry.

A scratching, faint but insistent, from beyond the closet door.

Federico leaped back, his mouth dry. "B-begone—"

More scratching. Federico would give half his country for a friend right now.

"Mrow. . . ."

"Oh, heavens." It was only a cat, trapped in this fancy carved closet. With a snort of relief, Federico sheathed his knife. "Come out," he called, lifting the latch.

A kitten thrust its way out, tail quivering. "Mrow?" A kitten as tawny as a lion, with black-tipped ears. He scooped her up, and she purred in his hands. Her amber eyes, lined in black like the kohl-rimmed eyes of Egyptians, shone in the lantern light. Her kitten teeth were no thicker than needles. "Mrow?"

"Greetings." Federico bowed. "I am Sir Federico Gonzaga, son of Duke Francesco II of Mantua and Lady Isabella d'Este of Ferrara."

"Mrow." The kitten reached out a paw as soft as a kiss to tap his nose, and wiggled to be free.

"Certainly, my lady. I would not detain you." Federico set her down, and she bounced across the floor, rolling like a jester—a far better jester than the one at the banquet! He laughed, clapping. He could spend the rest of his life watching this.

Abruptly she stopped to lick a paw as if to say *Me, tumble? Never!*

She spotted a bit of feather and crouched, creeping toward it. She sprang—

"Captured!" exclaimed Federico. "Oh, you are too clever."

She scrambled down the corridor with the determination of a tiny racehorse and careened back, bouncing off his ankles. "Mrow," she boasted, her whole body purring.

"A proper sprinter you are." Federico petted her. "Though we need to work on your turns."

The kitten pranced away—and suddenly her back arched, fur bristling, as she skittered on tiptoe toward him, hissing through her kitten teeth.

"Oh, you are fierce. I'm quite frightened." He hid behind his cloak, to demonstrate.

She batted at the cloak's hem, climbing his legs—

"Ow!" He laughed, setting her down. "These hose are silk."

She wandered toward the closet, batting the door. "Mrow?"

Federico jumped to open it. Sniffing the air, the kitten toddled in.

He closed the door with a bow—"My lady"—and threw it open. "For you."

No kitten emerged.

"Kitten?" He peered into the closet.

Nothing there.

Federico scrambled for the lantern. "Where are you?" He knelt, running his hands along the wood. He shone the lantern into the corners, onto the door with its gems. No kitten. Only strange symbols in black ebony and white holly wood.

He stepped back, panic rising. "Kitten?" Somewhere in the distance people laughed and strummed, but in this corridor: only silence. Silence, and the tolling bells of Santo Spirito.

A sob swelled in Federico's chest. "Where are you?" He should smash this closet to bits! Shatter the gems with the butt of his knife, then stomp on the fragments. Such strangeness wasn't right. "Kitten?"

The last notes of Santo Spirito faded to silence. The bells of Sant'Agostino began, and of Santa Rufina, for every church in Rome has its own version of midnight.

Federico gulped lungfuls of air. Was this a dreadful

prank? Witchcraft? Something evil. With great sadness he shut the closet door. "Goodbye, kitten." It would be a long walk indeed to the villa. The lantern hung from his hand like a hundred-pound weight. Never in his life had he felt so alone.

"Mrow."

He dashed back—threw open the door—

A cat sauntered out. A full-grown cat with a coat like a lion, her eyes lined in black. She gazed up at him. "Mrow?" she asked—but with a cat's voice, not a squeak.

"Kitten?" he whispered.

The cat threaded through his legs, rubbing his calves with black-tipped ears.

He gulped. "It's you. But how . . . ?"

"Mrow." She ambled toward the closet, her amber eyes winking in the lantern light. No more kitten tumbling. "Mrow?" She batted the door.

"No!" Federico snatched her up. "That thing's too dangerous." Clutching her to his chest, not caring who heard his footsteps, he ran as fast as he could back to his villa.

## Chapter 2
## INTERESTING INFORMATION

Federico awoke the next day filled with heartbreak. How sad that he'd dreamed of a friendly cat just for him! He rolled over, burying his face in the pillow.

"Mrow."

Federico's eyes flew open. There, on the mattress beside him: the cat's smiling face, and her warm purr. Suddenly all was right with the world.

The cat spent the morning with him, curled at his elbow as he sat at his desk scratching out a letter. This is what he managed:

*Dearest Mother. I continue in my lessons.*
*I hope you are doing well and also my sisters.*
*Master Raphael has finished my portrait. I have a cat.*
*Your devoted son, Federico*

He wanted to describe Michelangelo's strange midnight behavior and boast about beating the pope at backgammon. He very much wanted to tell his mother of the cat, how she had grown so quickly from a kitten, how she disappeared through a closet. . . . But he could not do any of these things because the letter was in Latin, and Latin for Federico was a toil.

"Should I say, 'I found you in the corridor at midnight'?" he asked.

"Mrow."

"You're right. Never mind." He studied his father's portrait above the desk—a scowling man with bobbed hair and round beard, his black armor trimmed in red. A great warrior. Federico would be a warrior, too, someday. Warriors didn't need Latin.

The cat rubbed his shoulder, purring. He smiled as he scratched the cat's ears. A wonderful notion came to him: he should give her a gift to show his love. So after Latin lessons were finished, and fencing lessons with his Señor Pedro, he made his way across the palace grounds to the stables, seeking out the saddler. A saddler crafted all sorts of leather goods for all sorts of creatures. Federico would purchase a decoration suitable for the pet of a gentleman.

With some caution, he approached the bench where the saddler worked, under an awning to protect him from the summer sun, the air thick with the scents of beeswax and leather and horses. Normally Federico avoided the saddler, who had a scarred cheek and constant sneer. Now, though, he steeled himself. "Excuse me, Master."

The saddler studied Federico as if the boy was a cowhide. "Yes, my lord?" The scar on his cheek tugged away his smile.

"I—I require a collar for a—a cat. A nice one, if you please."

The saddler laid down the bridle he'd been splicing to rummage through his bench. So many tools for piercing and cutting! He held up a strap of red leather trimmed in pearls. "This, my lord?"

Red and white were the Gonzaga colors! Federico bit his lip to keep from gasping—any display of interest would increase the cost. "Unless you've something better."

"Nothing so fine." The saddler turned the strap so the

pearls caught the light. "For you, my lord, I ask . . . three ducats."

This time Federico could not help his gasp. "I haven't got three ducats."

But the collar was so soft. So perfect.

The saddler eyed him sideways. "There is, my lord, one solution. Perhaps you damaged your jousting saddle. The repair will cost three ducats."

"But I've not damaged my saddle." Federico looked puzzled. "Have I?"

"Let us say you did. I write your mother's secretary. He pays me."

"Ah," said Federico, catching on. "And meanwhile, the collar would be mine."

"Precisely." Again the saddler's scar canceled his smile. "A gentleman gets others to pay his expenses."

How rude this man was. Federico should stomp away at the insult. But he very much wanted the collar. "See that it is done," he said finally—one of his mother's phrases. He pocketed the collar with his nose in the air, to teach the saddler a lesson. If only Federico had a friend to witness his cleverness. But such was his life in Rome.

Back in his bedroom, Federico hurried to present the collar to the cat, who preened at the attention. Sporting this gorgeous new adornment, she kept Federico company throughout his classes in French and oration and dance and watched like an elegant statue as Celeste dressed him for the evening's banquet.

"Look at you," the old woman declared, arranging a red and white cap on Federico's head. "As fine as your papa." She set his dress knife on his belt and a cloak lined in red silk across his shoulders.

"Mrow," the cat agreed, arching her neck to show off her own colors.

Federico beamed at their compliments.

"You do your family proud, my lord," Celeste stated. "One has no greater purpose than family."

The banquet, hosted by a cardinal and his nephew in a palazzo across the river, went very well indeed. The cardinal gifted Federico a charming silver saltcellar and even gave him the honor of carving the swan. The noblemen's wives, glittering with jewels, each told Federico how handsome he looked and how good he was to be the pope's *guest*. None of them used the word *hostage*. Most importantly, Federico learned that the strange wooden box in the corridor had been a present to the pope from the King of France.

He frowned, pondering. "Does the King of France have kittens?"

"Kittens?" a countess laughed, pinching his cheek. "I should say not, you witty boy."

Federico returned to the villa with his belly aching from too many tarts and his cheeks afire from pinching. The cat sat up when he entered, her amber eyes blinking. "What were you doing in a closet from France?" he asked, petting her. A closet from a king—how he wanted to study it. "Shall we go on an adventure?"

"Mrow," the cat answered, her pearl collar glimmering. *Of course,* she seemed to be saying.

And so, making sure Celeste was asleep, Federico set off with his pet, the moon so bright they did not need a lantern. The cat lounged in his embrace, watching the corridor's shadows with bright eyes. The statues in the garden below glowed with unearthly pallor; they seemed almost to sway in the moonlight. Moonlight flowed through the windows and unfinished roof, lighting the closet with its pearly glow.

The closet door did not hold gems, Federico could now

see—how silly he'd been. Instead, eight glass balls were set in the wood, at the tips of an eight-pointed star. The balls glowed slightly in the light. Above the star ran symbols, or possibly letters from an alphabet he did not know. It took skill indeed to inlay wood so perfectly.

Cautiously he opened the door. "Mrow!" the cat squeaked.

"Sorry." He'd been gripping her a bit tightly.

The closet's back wall, he now saw, held eight mirrors, set to catch the light from the balls. The back of the door contained a glass globe the size of an orange.

He touched the globe. Sloshing water had been sealed within. Several times he closed and opened the door, puzzling at the globe's strangeness, as the cat watched from his arms. The mirrors, he reckoned, reflected light from the balls into the water. But why would someone go to such effort to move light and catch it?

"Why not use a lantern?" he asked the cat.

"Mrow," she yawned.

He shut the door, frowning. It made no sense. Once again he eased it open. Inside the globe, water swirled.

Midnight bells broke the silence. Jerking in surprise, the cat leaped from his grip.

"Ow," Federico exclaimed, and "Stop!" as she jumped into the closet. He lunged after her, trying to grab her—

And then his fingers met cloth, and a leg, for a man was somehow stepping out of the closet into the corridor.

Federico stumbled back with a yelp of surprise.

"How you do?" the man asked in terrible Italian. He held a cat in his arms—Federico's cat! "I am much happy to meet you."

## Chapter 3

## CANDY, AND A FRIEND

The stranger was dressed like no one Federico had ever seen. His head was bare and his breeches drooped to his ankles, yet he grinned at the world as if he owned it. "Listen to bells!" he cried happily. "They ring midnight."

"Where's her collar?" Federico snapped, too angry now to be frightened. He pointed to the cat. "The red collar with pearls? It cost three ducats."

The man peered around the corridor. "Please to tell me, what is the date here?"

"Why, the year of our Lord 1511," Federico answered. What a ridiculous question. "Where's her collar?" he repeated.

The man grinned, petting the cat. "Look what you get me into, Juno." He caught sight of Federico's frown. "That is her name. Juno. The queen of gods."

"I know who Juno is," Federico retorted. "I read Latin."

"This is a nice house you have." How ill-mannered this man was! He spoke with the rudest of accents, he held the cat as if he owned her, and he didn't even bow.

"It is a palace," Federico corrected. "The Vatican Palace. It belongs to His Holiness, the pope."

"Oh," said the man. "You like I look around?"

"No." Federico could be ill mannered, too. An idea came to him, quite brilliant. "I mean, yes. Which is to say—come." Flipping his cloak, he led the stranger up the corridor. He'd show this nobody the meaning of importance.

"A lot of works are going on here," the man observed of the buckets and ladders cluttering the palace.

"Yes. His Holiness and I have many ideas." Federico waited, but the man did not even comment. "Here, for example, is His Holiness's new audience room." Moonlight caught the shining eyes of newly finished figures, the illusion of columns and trees.

The stranger's jaw dropped. "The paintings of Raphael!"

Setting down the cat, he dashed to an image of kneeling soldiers and leaned close, studying their uniforms.

"Those are Swiss Guards. They fight with swords and pikes, and are loyal till death."

"Mmm." The man's nose almost touched the wall. The cat wandered off, sniffing at shadows.

"We should continue. I have more to show. This next room shall be His Holiness's study—"

"*The School of Athens!*" The man beamed at Federico. The cat curled round Federico's ankles. "And look: you are friends with Juno."

Federico hurried to pick up the cat. "To tell you the truth, I haven't named her yet."

The man shrugged as he turned back to the painting. "Juno is the name from her master when she was a baby." He pointed to the rough platform edging the room. "May I?"

"Please." Federico lifted the cat—*his* cat—onto the platform and scrambled up. Suddenly he felt nervous. What if the stranger laughed? How Federico had yearned to show off his portrait. And yet—

"That one is Socrates." The man pointed to a figure. "Him

I know from university." He leaned in, studying a sandaled foot. "Oh, it is wonderful to see this so new."

Whatever *that* meant. "And this is Homer, and Pythagorus, and here . . ."

"Here what?" the man asked, his eyes bright. "Please tell me." He scanned the wall, admiring the draped togas, the Arab philosopher in a turban. . . . "It is you!" He gaped at the figure of a boy with blond curls, then spun to Federico. "His hair—his chin—his eyes! They are like stars."

"They *twinkle*," Federico clarified. "Raphael said they should."

The man touched the portrait. "Is amazing. Is perfect. Thank you for showing this me."

Federico shrugged, though inside he grinned like a jester. How could he ever have thought poorly of this man? "I'm sorry, but I did not catch your name. I am Sir Federico of Mantua."

"Pleased to meet you, Sir Federico. Herbert Bother of New Jersey. Call me Herbert."

"'Erbert . . . 'Erbert Botter." Federico worked his mouth around the strange syllables. Those irksome northern languages with their unpronounceable H names! Juno sat beside them licking a paw. *Juno.* Hmm. It was, he had to admit, a fine name, especially for a cat so regal. He would have thought of it eventually.

Herbert nodded in satisfaction as he admired the wall, even wiping his eyes with a handkerchief. "You like chocolate?" He grinned, stowing the cloth in a pocket.

"I'm afraid I do not know that word." Federico did not want to insult the man's Italian.

Herbert settled himself on the platform, pulling out two lumps wrapped in paper. "You'll like this, I am sure. It is candy." Juno curled round him affectionately.

"You mean sweets?" Federico plopped himself beside them. "I must confess I'm quite fond of confections."

"Yes. I, too." Herbert unwrapped one and handed it over.

Federico's heart sank. The brown lump was nothing but poo.

"It's delicious," Herbert reassured him, taking a bite. "Is called chocolate."

"Mrow," Juno announced. She might have been laughing.

Federico braved a nibble. The confection wasn't spicy or tangy or honey-flavored; it didn't feel gummy or chewy or hard; it did not smell of cordials or fruit. It was like nothing he'd ever tasted. It melted across his tongue like butter, but better.

Herbert watched, grinning from ear to ear. "You do not have chocolate in 1511?"

Federico shook his head. "I would know," he said thickly, taking another bite.

"In middle is surprise. Peanuts."

The most delectable nuts Federico had ever tasted! Chewy but not too chewy, and rich, and flavored with a scent that filled his nose in the nicest way. "Pea-nuts." He chewed, savoring. "Choc-o-late. You are correct, 'Erbert: this is delicious."

They ate with their feet dangling off the platform, Herbert's loose breeches so different from Federico's hose. "You speak Italian very well," Federico offered.

"You are too nice. I lived some in Italy to study painting." Herbert mimed a paintbrush. "As an artist, I am bad. But also I buy art to sell in my country. I buy—what is the word? Sketches."

"Just sketches?" Federico smiled as Juno sniffed his fingers. "Not the artists' finished work?"

"Yes. From all sorts of artists—" Herbert froze mid-bite. He turned to stare at the vast wall behind them. Slowly his gaze returned to Federico. "You . . ." He swallowed. "You know Raphael."

"Naturally. I saw him yesterday, in fact." Federico looked pointedly at Herbert's pocket. "The chocolate was extremely delicious." Perhaps Herbert had another piece.

Herbert scratched his cheek. "Listen, Sir Federico. What do you say to a business? You bring me sketches—the little garbages that artists make. I pay you in chocolate."

"Hmm. I might be interested." Federico made a show of shrugging as he scratched Juno's ears. For a few scraps of paper, he'd get the most delicious food in the world! He pointed to a stack of papers in a corner. "How much chocolate might I—might one—get for those?"

"My golly!" Herbert jumped off the platform, startling Juno. He riffled through the pages: a foot, a hand, a curl of hair . . . all the details that make up a finished painting. "These are wonderful."

With a lash of her tail, Juno leaped down. "Mrow!" she complained, pacing at the study door.

"Juno!" Federico scrambled after her. "Be careful."

"Is late for her. Golly, is late for you, too! Don't your mama and papa worry?"

"My parents do not live in Rome." Federico sighed. "To tell the truth, I'm a hostage. My father leads the pope's army, and His Holiness does not want the French hiring him away."

Herbert looked horrified. "But you are only a little one. That is terrible!"

"It is, sometimes." Herbert's voice was so kind that Federico found a lump in his throat. "I miss my sisters. They would love exploring this place with me. They'd love chocolate."

"But who is here to keep you safe?"

"Mrow!" Juno glared at them from the door.

"Juno." Federico couldn't help grinning. "And Celeste, and my tutors." But now Herbert had him worried. If Celeste found his bed empty . . . "I should go."

Herbert, too, got to his feet. "I am sorry that you are away from your family. But I am happy to meet you! You come back again at midnight? That is when the closet works. I come back, too. With chocolate."

"Not only chocolate." Federico paused in the doorway. "Chocolate and peanuts."

"Chocolate and peanuts." Herbert chuckled. "Until tomorrow, my friend."

And with that wonderful promise ringing in his ears,

Federico dashed off, Juno beside him. Together they reached the corridor, leaping puddles of moonlight as they galloped.

"Mrow," Juno sang, sprinting ahead.

"Wait up," Federico called, in the manner that one called to a friend. Juno was his friend. Juno, and Herbert, however they had appeared. Two friends he had now, and the promise of chocolate!

## Chapter 4

## RUMORS OF DA VINCI AND THIEVES

Though he awoke barely rested, Federico could not stop smiling. Wasn't Juno a clever pet, bringing him Herbert? Most cats brought only dead mice. He kissed her in delight.

"Come, come." Celeste scuttled in, clapping her hands. "Saints above, that cat delays you. What if you are late for His Holiness?"

At once Federico's joy doubled, for today would require his very best clothes. He had a ceremony to attend at the palace, followed by dinner and an opera. "I shall find a drawing or two," he whispered to Juno, "to trade for chocolate and peanuts."

"What are you saying?" Celeste scrubbed his cheek. "Is this mud?" She continued grumbling but Federico was too busy dreaming of chocolate to listen. She brought him to the mirror. "Look at you," she clucked. "An angel, you are."

Federico studied the image smiling back at him in the costly Venetian glass. White silk doublet, a jerkin of white brocade, a gold-threaded cloak, and his white velvet cap with diamond trim . . . He did indeed look like an angel. "Aren't I fine, Juno?" He reached to pet her, but Celeste slapped his hand away.

"She'll shed on your beautiful clothes. Now hurry. We shan't have His Holiness calling you tardy."

And so Federico trotted off for the palace. The sun twinkled, the buckles on his slippers twinkled, his rings twinkled—all was right with the world. He admired the pope's garden through the windows as he strode the corridor, the marble statues gleaming between the trees. Two broad-shouldered Swiss Guards marched the grounds, their striped costumes as bright as jewels. Across the corridor, the windows overlooked the city's red rooftops and wide lazy river.

Federico passed a niche with a little locked door—the private entrance to Michelangelo's studio. Perhaps the unhappy man toiled there even now. At least the corridor didn't smell.

He reached the strange closet. Though midnight was hours away, he bravely cracked open the door. "'Erbert?" he whispered, but the closet was empty. How, he wondered, had Herbert appeared here? He could not see space enough to hide a spider, let alone a full-grown man such as Herbert. He closed the door with a bit of a shudder. The King of France should send normal presents such as horses or dogs.

Finally, Federico reached the palace and the pope's stateroom, jammed with a tremendous buzzing crowd.

"Sir Federico!" His Holiness roared. "Look at him," he exclaimed to the French ambassador. Standing next to the ambassador, the pope looked like a barrel beside a reed, for he was a man of some girth. "Such a fine young fellow. He's like a grandson to me." The pope pretended to box. "You want to fight me, young man? You want to fight?"

Federico forced a laugh. "That is funny." Even joking, the pope punched hard. "I have been admiring your new closet, Your Holiness." Federico should offer a compliment.

"Eh?" The pope looked past him, scanning the room. A Spanish cardinal had just arrived.

"The gift from the King of France—"

"What? We'll talk later." And off the pope went, quite abandoning Federico.

"Ze nerve of zat man," the ambassador sputtered.

Federico glanced toward the pope's private office. Would anyone notice if he slipped inside? He needed to find some sketches for Herbert—

"You like ze closet, eh?" The French ambassador interrupted Federico's musings. "You have good taste. It was designed by Master Leonardo."

Federico's jaw dropped. "Leonardo da Vinci?" This genius, as everyone knew, now worked for the King of France. But he had lived for a time in the Gonzaga castle. "He drew my mother's portrait." And she had been pestering him ever since to finish it. All his life, Federico had heard her complaints on this subject.

"I have seen zat portrait." The ambassador studied Federico. "Ze closet. . . . I tell you. Da Vinci had an idea to send things through ze air, or somezing." He waved a hand. "But zere was an accident, and he refuse to work anymore. So ze king has only a very expensive box. Voilà, a gift for ze pope."

"An accident?" Federico breathed. No wonder the closet seemed so ominous. "What happened?"

"He does not say. No—zat is not true." The ambassador leaned close, his eyebrows so high that they disappeared under his cap. "He says five words: 'I have lost little Juno.'"

The hair stood up on Federico's neck. "Juno?"

The ambassador grinned at Federico. "You are good spy, eh? I would not tell zis to a man. But to a child—"

Alas, Federico could not learn more, for at that moment the master of ceremonies whistled everyone to attention, to start the procession to the chapel. Dutifully Federico stood where he was told, his mind awhirl. Dutifully he marched into the Sistine Chapel behind His Holiness (who was carried in upon a chair, as the pope should be), and dutifully he sat in a place befitting the heir to Mantua. The chapel ceiling was being painted, yes. But clever Michelangelo had designed the scaffolding so that the floor of the chapel remained free while he worked, and hundreds of worshippers now filled the space. The ceiling soared above their heads: half unpainted gray stucco, the other half protected by an enormous canvas cloth to catch drips of paint and keep the work secret. Against one wall stood a ladder that Federico had climbed often, for his mother insisted on hearing of Michelangelo's progress.

The chattering quieted as the service began. His Holiness

promptly went to sleep, as he usually did during ceremonies. Federico could not hear the priests for the pope's snoring, but it did not matter because he had so much to ponder.

The great Leonardo da Vinci had designed the closet? How remarkable. And Juno—why, she must be da Vinci's cat. Somehow, she traveled from France to Rome while only a kitten. Then she'd vanished back into that closet to return fully grown, and return again with Herbert. But how?

*Aha,* thought Federico. *Herbert is Leonardo da Vinci.*

But no, that was impossible. Leonardo da Vinci dressed beautifully; everyone knew this. And he spoke perfect Italian. And he knew what year it was, for heaven's sake.

Perhaps Herbert was a servant of Leonardo da Vinci?

The great man would not hire someone so ignorant.

Perhaps Herbert knew the King of France? No.

It was all so puzzling.

Federico wished he had a friend to talk to and figure this out. But the obvious person—the only person, really—was Herbert.

At last the service ended, His Holiness awakening with a snort. The crowd surged around the pope like goats round a bucket of grain, all hoping for a blessing or a word. Federico followed the flock out of the chapel and back to the state-room, greeting various canons and bishops and secretaries, knights and marquises and counts. Everyone wanted to compliment his outfit and his family, and he must display flawless manners. So he waited, a perfect gentleman, while keeping an eye on the door to the pope's private office. He must get a sketch for Herbert!

Slowly he edged nearer. On the far side of the room, His Holiness roared at some jest, and the crowd as one turned to look. Now was Federico's chance. With a deep breath to stifle his panic, he eased the door open and slipped in.

What a treasure trove. Shelves crammed with globes and books and statuettes lined the room. An open cabinet revealed rolls of building plans. A ledge held piles of sketches. Hurriedly Federico flipped through. What would Herbert like? A fat cherub carrying grapes? A donkey peering into the manger? A smiling woman with soft curling hair? He paused at a pen-and-ink drawing of a bearded old man, signed by Michelangelo. Perhaps it was a portrait of His Holiness—which explained its place at the bottom of the pile! The pope did not fancy himself old. Federico would be doing him a favor to remove it.

———

Hastily unbuttoning his doublet, Federico slipped the drawing underneath. This was not stealing, he assured himself—certainly not. Gentlemen never stole. But still, the less said, the better.

The door opened as Federico was smoothing the last button. He jumped like a fish on a hook.

A Swiss Guard in a velvet uniform peered in. Like all Swiss Guards, he was terrifying. "Forgive me, my lord." He bowed, his hand yet on the hilt of his sword. "I did not mean to interrupt."

Federico struggled to appear calm. He was the son of the Duke of Mantua, after all, and a guest of His Holiness. The pope himself had promised Federico free use of the palace. Did not *free use* include the pope's office? "Think—think nothing of it," he stuttered.

The guard studied Federico. "Are you felling unwell?"

Again Federico smoothed his doublet. "I simply needed a moment of quiet." One of his mother's favorite expressions. He eased past the guard, heart hammering against his ribs.

Once back in the stateroom, his anxiety did not ease, for the mood had shifted. In the few minutes Federico was absent, something terrible must have happened. *I am caught,* he thought in panic—

But no, he was not, for none of the guests even looked at him.

He eased his way into the crowd. "Pray tell, what has happened?" he whispered to the French ambassador.

The ambassador leaned in, eyebrows high. "Zere is a thief in ze palace."

"A thief?" Federico kept one hand on his doublet.

"Zat is ze truth." The ambassador's voice dropped. "Raphael's papers were stolen. Every last one."

## Chapter 5

## A Satisfying Trade

As the church bells tolled midnight, Federico paced the corridor clutching the sketch of the bearded old man. All evening he'd fretted as he sat through a tedious dinner and even more tedious opera. What if someone realized he had taken this drawing? What if he were connected to Raphael's missing papers? What if Herbert did not return, and Federico never again tasted chocolate?

So when Herbert at last stepped out of the closet, Federico felt not relief or joy but only irritation. "Here," he snapped. "A Michelangelo."

"Oh, it is beautiful!" Herbert took the drawing, cradling

it like a precious jewel. "Oh, my." He squatted by Federico's lantern to study the old man's thick brows and thoughtful frown. "And look, it is signed. Thank you." He beamed at Federico. "You thief this?"

Federico frowned. "Never!" He had given this matter no small amount of thought in the hours of dinner and opera. "I am here in Rome as a guest of His Holiness. A host should treat guests well and give them presents. That"—he jerked his chin at the drawing—"is a present. A gift I have given myself, as a guest. And now I give it to you."

Herbert nodded thoughtfully. "That makes much logic." He settled himself on a stack of planks next to the closet, easing the drawing into his bag. "It is good you are not a thief."

"No, I'm not. But what about you?" Federico crossed his arms, still irked. "You took those Raphaels, didn't you? You need to return them."

"I cannot," Herbert sighed. One by one he removed chocolates from his bag, each piece half the size of a fist. "They make me too much money." He motioned for Federico to join him.

Well. Federico should continue his scolding, but he must test these candies first. After a bit of a pause to demonstrate that he was not entirely pleased, he sat on the planks, placing the lantern between him and Herbert. Deliberately he selected the second-largest piece and took a nibble. How delicious the peanuts tasted. Even better than he remembered.

"It came from Mantua, you know," Herbert said through a mouthful of chocolate.

Blinking at the interruption, Federico followed Herbert's pointing finger. "That closet came from Mantua?"

Herbert nodded. "I buy it in a junk shop—a shop that sells rubbish. An old wooden trunk. I bring it back to my home. I take it apart, and inside I find beautiful wood." Herbert gestured at the star on the door. "Later, in a library in Paris—a private library—I read a notebook by Leonardo da Vinci, a notebook about a closet machine." He shook his head at the memory.

Federico listened, chocolate forgotten.

"So I follow his notes and turn the trunk back into a closet. And out walks a kitten."

"Juno," Federico whispered.

Herbert nodded. "Da Vinci even writes of her in his notebook."

"The kitten came here, too. She played with me." Federico

frowned. "Then she went back into the closet and came out a cat."

"That was when she was in New Jersey, with me. Such a wonderful kitten, eh? I have her for two years, then—"

"Two years?" Federico could not believe it. "But she was gone for only a minute!"

"In your time it was a minute. But not in mine." Herbert shook his head. "That is how the closet works. But then by mistake I leave the door open. In she goes . . . and comes back with a collar! By the way—" He held out three worn ducats.

"Ah." Federico had rather forgotten about the red collar with pearls. "Thank you."

"Do not use them for some years, however. They have a date of 1518."

"That's impossible." Herbert was speaking one bit of nonsense after another. Still, Federico could not help checking the coins in the lantern light.

Suddenly he felt very cold. "H-how did you get these?"

"I buy them from a man who sells antiques."

"But they're not antiques." Federico rubbed the coins, their edges smoothed by countless fingers. "Antiques are hundreds of years old."

"Yes." Herbert took a deep breath. "These coins are hundreds of years old. I come from hundreds of years away. From the year 1928, from a country called America."

"America?" Federico had never heard of it. "That doesn't make sense. People can't travel between times."

"To you, no. To me, no. But to the great inventor Leonardo da Vinci? Yes." Herbert nodded at the closet. "He made this. A machine for lookers."

"Lookers?" Federico had no idea what Herbert was talking about.

"You know. They come, they look"—Herbert pretended to peer about—"they learn secrets. That is why it works at midnight. Midnight is the time for lookers."

Not *lookers*, Federico realized with dawning horror. "You mean spies." He stared at the closet. "It's a machine for spies. You're a spy!"

Herbert chuckled. "No, I am only a man from New Jersey."

America? Zhersey? What *were* these places? "But—but— how . . . ?"

"It makes you cuckoo, yes, trying to figure this out?" Herbert took another chocolate. "This is what I think. Da Vinci wanted a machine to move people from one place to another place. To spy in the night. But somehow the machine moves you from one time to another time. And when you go back"— he snapped his fingers—"no time passes. I return the very moment I leave. Juno, too. I live my life in America, I do my jobs, and when I am ready, I come here. At midnight."

Federico shivered—and not from the breeze dancing through the windows. This did indeed make one cuckoo.

"By the way, what do you think?" Herbert patted his jerkin. "Do you like?"

Federico had been so busy with chocolate and talk of the closet that he hadn't even noticed Herbert's clothes. Heavens, the man was sporting a jerkin! In fact, Herbert's entire outfit looked familiar, nothing like his strange garb last night. Familiar . . . but wrong. His cap was out of style by a decade, his hose were striped (striped! In 1511!), and his shoes were fit only for Germans.

"I am in fashion now, yes?"

Federico picked his words diplomatically, as his mother would. "Ah. Interesting."

"So now we can walk in the palace together, and meet Raphael!"

"Heavens, no," Federico blurted. *Raphael?* Herbert did not even have a belt.

Herbert's face fell. "But I study many months to get this right. I pay a tailor. Please, Federico. I must see Raphael. And I want—I hope!—to see the Sistine Chapel."

"Alas, the chapel is locked." Federico eyed the last chocolate. Could he take half?

"How much candy you want?" Herbert asked suddenly.

Federico paused mid-reach. "I beg your pardon?"

"If I dress right, you take me to art. Yes?" Herbert pointed to his clothes. "So how can you fix this?"

Federico studied him as a sculptor might study a block of marble. "Well, the cap, for starters. One sees beggars in caps like that, but no one in the palace. Certainly not a gentleman. And the hose? Ugh." He tugged at Herbert's cloak. "You're wearing this wrong. If you cover the jerkin, it's not so bad. The shoes, however . . ." He made a show of frowning, but inside he bubbled with joy. "I warn you, 'Erbert: this will take a lot of chocolate."

## Chapter 6
## FEDERICO VISITS A MADMAN

The next day, Federico hurried through Greek and French and Latin while Juno purred in his lap. Thanks to her assistance, he was finished by early afternoon—plenty of time to visit the Sistine Chapel. It would take all his skill to manage Michelangelo. He wished he could bring Herbert's three ducats, for the sculptor loved money almost as much as art. Juno, beautiful even without a collar, would accompany him. "Be your most charming," he instructed.

"Mrow," she cried, her tail swaying. *How fun to visit the palace together!*

Soon into their journey, they encountered yet another

treat: Master Raphael, passing through the villa with his usual parade of friends and students and admirers. "Sir Federico," the painter cried, swooping into a bow. "The gentleman who dances like a Frenchman and rides like a Spaniard. I've missed your handsome face."

Federico adjusted his doublet, blushing with pride. "Good day, Master Raphael."

The artist stooped to stroke Juno. "What a gorgeous creature. So full of love." He chuckled. "Did you hear that Michelangelo has been to the pope's new study to see your portrait? Though he'd die before admitting it."

Federico did his best to look surprised. "Truly? How do you know?"

"The smell, of course." Raphael shook his head. "That man has a bakery's worth of genius while I have only crumbs."

"Far more than crumbs," Federico assured him. "And I'm sorry about your missing sketches." For he was sorry, however much the sketches helped Herbert.

"'Tis no matter." Raphael smiled. "I shall simply draw more. Come!" he announced to his parade. "Or we'll miss the architect." The parade marched off.

"Well, you certainly charmed one artist." Federico laughed,

petting Juno. "Hopefully Michelangelo will be so easy." He beamed at the promise of showing Michelangelo's masterpiece to Herbert. All he needed was the key. How hard could that be?

They headed up the corridor. Juno scampered ahead, leaping onto stacks of tile like a dragon conquering castles. Why, Federico wondered, did Michelangelo hate Raphael so much? Raphael was absolutely perfect. Thoughtful, courteous, wise, a gentleman in every way. Federico wanted to be exactly like him, with just as many friends, when he had eight and twenty years. Even Juno walked with an extra swing to her tail; Raphael had enchanted her as well. Nimbly she climbed a ladder, swiping at Federico's cap as he walked by. She raced to the niche with its little locked door. "Mrow," she commanded, batting it with a paw.

Federico lifted her up. "That's the door to Michelangelo's studio. He doesn't like anyone going in there, not even you." He held her tightly as they walked past the closet. "I don't want you ending up back in that Zhersey place. I like you too much here."

"Mrow," Juno agreed, stretching her neck to be scratched, and she remained in his arms even when they entered the palace and its hubbub of construction.

At last they reached the grand doors of the Sistine Chapel—doors half as big as the wall. For a moment Federico feared the doors were locked, but no: only heavy. "Best behavior," he warned Juno, setting her down so he could push. More than once he'd had the privilege of watching Michelangelo at work, the artist standing with his head tipped back, his brush darting between a dozen pots of color. What a miracle, seeing feet and fabric and faces emerge from the wet plaster on the ceiling. Perhaps that might happen today.

Slowly the door opened, revealing the vast chapel with the canvas draped above, shafts of sun lighting the distant unfinished ceiling. Michelangelo's assistants scurried across the floor, gathering up snowflakes that drifted and spiraled through the air.

Juno sprang into the room, joyfully batting at the nearest flakes. Federico stared in shock, then dashed forward. "Juno! Stop!" These were not snowflakes that fell from the ceiling: they were bits of paper. He snatched a scrap: a penciled elbow. The next scrap contained lines he could not make out.

"Burn them!" shouted Michelangelo from above. "Burn everything."

"No!" cried Federico, grabbing the bits.

"Who is that? Who has entered? Is it the peacock?"

"No, Master," an assistant called. "'Tis only the young lord. Sir Federico."

Federico dashed to the far end of the chapel, waving up at the scaffolding. "Hello! I have come to show you my cat." He pointed to Juno leaping at the scraps. Perhaps she'd charm Michelangelo, too, or calm him at least.

Michelangelo peered over the edge. "Did you bring any humans?"

"No, Master. Might I come up?" *Stop ripping your drawings,* he wanted to scream. But one did not order Michelangelo.

"Hmph. Lock the door." Michelangelo stomped back into the shadows.

Federico decided that this meant yes and carefully began to climb. The scaffolding stood forty feet above the chapel floor, and he did not want to fall.

"Well? What is it?" Michelangelo snapped as Federico reached the top.

Federico eased himself onto the scaffolding, away from the edge. Forty feet was high indeed. "What are you doing?"

Michelangelo tore a drawing to shreds. "I don't want them stolen. There's a thief in the palace—haven't you heard?"

Federico's heart stopped. "It was a gift to myself—" he blurted.

"You took the peacock's sketches?"

Oh—Michelangelo did not know about Federico and the sketch of the bearded old man. Hastily he backtracked. "Which is to say I was hoping they would be a gift—before they were stolen. Perhaps there's another explanation—"

"Hmph." Michelangelo hurled down scraps. Far below, Juno swiped them across the floor. The assistants piled the shreds into baskets. "He stole from me in Florence and he'll steal from me here. He wants naught more than to mimic me." Michelangelo snatched up another handful.

"You are destroying your own work to keep Raphael from seeing it?" Federico asked helplessly.

"Yes!" Michelangelo spoke as though this truth were obvious.

Federico resisted grabbing his arm. "Master, I could take them."

"Why?" Michelangelo glared, his head cocked like a chicken. "To sell for silver coins?"

"Certainly not!" Federico dealt in chocolate, not grubby cash. "Your drawings are precious." Herbert would love every one.

"They are not precious. They are drafts." Michelangelo reached for another sheet. "An artist does not share doodles. An artist displays only genius." He gestured to the ceiling. "Behold."

Above Federico's head, two cherubs watched an old woman reading a book. Federico had seen the artist paint the folds of her robe, the cloth glowing like sunset. Even her grumpy old face came alive under Michelangelo's touch. "It's genius," Federico agreed. How to phrase the next bit? "I'd love to show it to someone."

"Who? An 'artist'? I am the only artist I know."

"He's a friend." How fine it felt, saying *friend*. "I'd show him when you're not here—with your key—"

"Never." Michelangelo tore up another handful. "Three thousand ducats, His Holiness pays me to paint this ceiling!"

"As you've said many times," Federico sighed. "That is far more than any other artist earns—"

"'Tis nothing," he snarled. "Everyone takes, and no one gives. Why are you here?"

"Yes—but—" It didn't matter. Michelangelo would never help him. "Good day, Master."

"Hmph." Michelangelo threw the handful of scraps off the

scaffolding. Even Juno had grown weary of the blizzard and sat washing her ears.

Federico edged his way down the ladder and trudged past the assistants still gathering shreds. He'd have to walk all the way back to the villa with nothing to show for his efforts.

Juno trotted over, her tail high. He scooped her up sadly.

"Mrow," she purred. *It's no matter. You have me.*

"You're right." Federico smiled. "I do." Together they passed through the magnificent palace to the corridor, his footsteps echoing in that long and empty space. The trees in the garden stood silent beneath the hot sun; even the statues looked lonely. But with Juno, he would never be alone again.

## Chapter 7
## A Difficult Journey

Federico awoke to darkness, the villa quiet. He'd slept through both horsemanship and dinner. Judging by the moon, it must be close to midnight. "I've nothing to bring 'Erbert," he told Juno sadly, keeping his voice low because of Celeste. The day's disappointments came flooding back, and the horrible memory of Michelangelo shredding his work. Federico had not rescued even a scrap.

"Mrow." Juno trotted after him to the door.

He deposited her back on the bed, stroking her golden fur. "It's not safe for you out there. What if you go through the closet?"

"Mrow," she agreed, draping herself across the bedspread. Idly she watched him depart with his lantern in hand, as the first bells of Santo Spirito marked midnight.

Federico reached the closet just as Herbert emerged grinning like a drunkard. "Behold, I am handsome!" he cried, for he had followed Federico's instructions to the letter. His hose were a fine snug brown, his boots neither too pointed nor too round. A black silk cloak hung from one shoulder, and his slashed doublet revealed its red lining. Even his bag met the latest style.

"You are indeed," Federico agreed, plucking the feather from Herbert's cap.

"What are you doing? That cost me a dollar."

"It's too Sicilian. Heavens, 'Erbert, you have a beard!" He had gray hair, too, and wrinkles at the corners of his eyes. "How long have you been gone?"

"Twelve years I have been living in New Jersey."

"Twelve *years*?" Federico shot a panicked glance at the closet. What sort of wickedness did that machine produce?

"I know, it is too much time. I missed you very much. But I had so much work! I make art, I sell art, I buy a house—I buy a house, Sir Federico, with the money from the Raphaels!"

"Those scraps of paper were worth an entire house?" Federico was stunned.

"A big house, with a room just for the closet." Herbert frowned. "Too big for only one person . . ." He shook himself and smiled. "But look—I have a job for us to do. I show you." He took a drawing from his bag—a small, perfect sketch of a boy with shoulder-length dark curls and a face full of sadness.

Federico gasped. "That's by Raphael. I'm sure of it."

"I am sure also. But he did not sign it, so no one believes me."

"Where did you get this?" Federico could not take his eyes off the drawing. The boy looked so alive yet so unhappy that he himself wanted to weep. One corner had the words *Age eleven.* Federico's age. How curious.

"In that." Herbert nodded at the closet. "In the trunk I buy in Mantua. It was hidden inside. I need Raphael to sign it." Carefully he returned the drawing to his bag. "So let us go to Raphael's house."

"Now?" Federico shook his head. "I can't leave the palace grounds in daytime, not without guards. At midnight? Never."

Herbert set off up the corridor. "Then I go alone. I know where his house is. I studied it."

Federico grabbed the lantern to hurry after him. "You're going into the city? You'll die."

Herbert opened the heavy door to the palace. "I take the stairs and turn left to a gate—"

"The city is too dangerous! You don't understand." He trailed Herbert, trying to convince him. "'Erbert, stop, please—" Hastily he backed up, pressing Herbert into the shadows, as footsteps tromped toward them. As quick as he could, he shuttered the lantern.

A guard approached—a Swiss Guard as big as an alp. He wore a sword, and the standard steel helmet, and the rich velvet cloth of a guardsman. Beneath the helmet's brim, his blue eyes glinted like ice. Onward he marched, glancing left and right—but he did not seem to notice Federico and Herbert in the depths of the stairs.

Silently Federico exhaled.

"There." Herbert pointed in the direction from which the guard had come. "It is a gate to the city."

"Please do not do this, 'Erbert. I'm sure the gate is locked."

But it was only latched, and Herbert opened it easily. A small gate for tradesmen, abandoned at this hour. "I must do this, Sir Federico. It is my fortune." Squinting through the darkness, he stepped out into the street.

Federico danced with indecision. As a guest of His Holiness—a hostage, a prisoner—Federico must not leave the palace! The midnight city swarmed with murderers and thieves. If evil men found him, he'd be held for ransom, or worse. Besides, departing the palace would look like fleeing.

But Herbert did not have a weapon. Not even a lantern. And Herbert was his friend. Alone, he might die. But Federico had knowledge and a light and a knife. And courage, yes? It took courage to walk through Rome. Raphael's house was not far. If they walked very fast . . .

With a soft muttered prayer, he stepped through the gate, following Herbert.

Immediately blackness pressed round. Noises seeped through the night: bellows, snarls, slams. A beggar cried for food. Federico kept close to Herbert, holding his knife loosely as Señor Pedro had taught him. One gripped at the last minute, for the thrust. He very much hoped he would not have to thrust.

Herbert hurried, clutching his bag. "What in tarnation?" he gasped, clamping his nose.

Federico sniffed. Rotting food. The waste of horses and cattle and people. The stink of the river and of the hospital. An animal carcass. Bad wine. "It's Rome."

Herbert paused, his head cocked. Mosquitos whined, a child wheezed . . . footsteps.

"Don't stop!" Federico whispered as the footsteps drew closer.

Herbert remained motionless, listening.

Now Federico could hear the snick of a sword being drawn. Frantically he tugged Herbert's cloak. "'Erbert!"

Herbert knelt in the muck of the street. A child lay in the gutter—a child Federico's age, perhaps, but so thin. "Water . . ." she gasped, reaching for them.

"'Erbert, we must move—"

Herbert stroked back the girl's hair. "Where is your mama?" He glared at Federico. "Where's her mama?"

"It doesn't matter!" Federico knew too well the signs of death. He'd watched his sister Livia perish, taken by God with only six years. "We must move—"

A voice rumbled through the darkness: "My lord."

Panicked, Federico jabbed wildly with his knife—

The Swiss Guard emerged from the shadows. "You left the palace?" He snatched up Federico by his jerkin. "Are you mad?"

"Water, please," the girl coughed.

"I'm not fleeing, I am only—" Federico babbled. "We were just—Raphael—"

Herbert lifted the girl, her rags smearing his cloak. "We must help."

A scream ripped through the darkness. Someone somewhere, shrieking.

"Leave her," the guard snapped at Herbert, holding his sword against the shadows.

"My neighbor is doctor. He can help." Herbert hurried toward the palace.

Another scream, closer.

"Stop!" the guard ordered, hauling Federico along. "He cannot do that."

"I know!" One did not bring a beggar into the pope's palace. "'Erbert—" Federico called.

Herbert sprinted, the beggar-girl in his arms. Bag flapping, he elbowed his way through the gate.

The Swiss Guard shoved Federico into the palace, his eyes darting everywhere. "What is he doing? He'll bring sickness and death upon us!"

"Don't worry." Federico tried to catch his breath. "He's going somewhere safe."

"Safe? 'Tis my head!" The guard struggled to lock the gate. "Go!" he barked. "Find them!"

Federico darted through the hallways, catching up to Herbert only in the corridor. Herbert struggled to open the closet door as the girl drooped, eyes closed.

"You must live, child!" Herbert shook her. "Federico, she must live!"

Federico reached around Herbert to open the door. He looked down at the girl, so pale in the moonlight. Wisps of hair clung to her forehead. A memory came to him of Livia tossing with fever. . . . Without warning, a sob caught in his chest. "Take care of her, 'Erbert."

"I will try. Goodbye, my friend." Herbert stepped into the closet. He was gone.

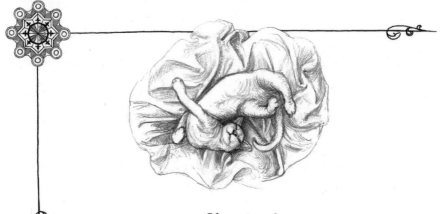

## Chapter 8
## A GUEST OF HIS HOLINESS

That night Federico dreamed of Livia sprawled in her sick-bed. He awoke with a gasp, and at once prayed that God keep her preserved in heaven. She must be very happy there, he comforted himself, with lovely scents and no sickness to harm her. He said a prayer, too, for the beggar child, who had doubtless passed through heaven's gates. He was glad Herbert had money to bury her properly. His mother sometimes paid for beggars' funerals; now Herbert was doing the same.

Federico passed the entire day in the villa—he had no wish to encounter that angry Swiss Guard—and perked up only at sunset as he and Celeste picked out his clothes. He was to spend the evening playing backgammon with His Holiness, and so must dress with special care. Naturally he wore his black cloak with violet lining—a gift from the pope—matched with black breeches and hose. Celeste strapped on Federico's gold-trimmed belt as his Latin tutor hovered uselessly, blathering. Master Sniffly, Federico called him, though only when no one could hear.

"Has he read my new poem?" Master Sniffly asked, dabbing at his nose. "Please beg him to."

Juno yawned as she lounged on the bed. To Federico, she seemed to be snorting.

Celeste tugged a brush through Federico's curls. "And observe whether His Holiness's cuffs are double pleated. The tailor wants to know."

"The poem has fifty-two stanzas," Master Sniffly continued, "for each week of the year. The week of his birthday I emphasized especially."

Juno yawned again.

At last these two gnats finished their buzzing. With a kiss to Juno, Federico trotted up the corridor to the palace, though he turned away as he passed the closet. He'd visit that strange contraption soon enough. He decided that he must win every backgammon game so that His Holiness sent him away in frustration. Then he'd have more time with Herbert.

With a deep bow, he entered the pope's parlor. "Your Holiness, I so look forward—"

"Sir Federico." His Holiness slouched at the backgammon table; he did not even look up. "Look who I've invited to join us." Across from him sat a man equally white-haired and stout: Donato Bramante, the architect of the palace. He gave Federico a token bow.

Federico nodded coolly back. "Good evening, Master." He should have expected that Bramante would be here. The architect found every opportunity to curry favor with His Holiness.

"Pour for us, my boy," Bramante ordered, jangling his key ring as he studied the board. He was forever flaunting his keys to display his access to the palace.

Federico stiffened. How dare Bramante, the son of a farmer, order around a Gonzaga! But Federico caught himself just in time. Bramante carried a key to the Sistine Chapel. If Federico could somehow get to the architect's key ring, he could unlock the chapel for Herbert. He could at last share Michelangelo's masterpiece with his friend. "Certainly,

Master. In fact, allow me to serve the whole meal."

And so all that night Federico waited on the two men, carving the goose as he had been taught, carrying in the roast lamb on its heavy silver tray, ladling the nutmeg sauce and the saffron sauce and the parsley sauce that was now so popular.

"Your—Holiness," Bramante burped, "what—you think of yer—garden?"

Federico stood over the architect, refilling his plate. "I should very much like to see your key collection," he said boldly. Perhaps he could extract the Sistine Chapel key somehow.

"Is not—for little boys." Bramante patted the key ring as he speared an onion tart. "Zounds—we eat—a lot."

"Enough twaddle about keys," His Holiness muttered, mopping at the sauce.

Federico scowled as he carried out an empty tray.

"Are they quite right in there?" puffed the wine steward, unloading another armful of bottles. "We don't want His Holiness falling asleep."

Aha! That was an idea. "He is fine," Federico assured him, taking a bottle and a platter of marzipan. He returned to the parlor. "Your Holiness? Master Architect? Allow me to entertain you with a recitation of Virgil."

How disappointed Master Sniffly would have been in his performance. As great as the writings of Virgil might be, and however dramatic the battle between Aeneas and his enemies, Federico spoke with the dull singsong of a mother rocking her babies. "Sed cadet," he droned, topping their glasses. "Ante diem mediaque. . . ."

His Holiness's head sagged on his chest.

Bramante took a fistful of marzipan. "Is that—Latin? I don't speak—Latin."

"Ante diem mediaque," Federico repeated, even more slowly.

His Holiness began to snore.

Bramante's head dropped to the table. He lay facedown in the parsley sauce, still clutching a sweet.

As silent as a breeze, Federico approached. Only a few minutes till midnight! *"These are my final words,"* he murmured in Latin. *"I spill them with my blood."* He reached under Bramante's cloak, unclasping the key ring. *"Rise from my ashes, children, and wreak vengeance."* Slipping off a heavy iron key, he returned the ring. *"No peace on sea, nor on land."*

Bramante lifted his head. "Wha?" he snorted.

Federico froze, key in hand. *"Battle forever, my sons. . . ."*

"No—Latin—" Bramante fell back onto the table.

Grabbing a lantern, Federico tiptoed out of the parlor. Wait till he told Herbert! Already Saint Mary Major rang midnight. He had no time at all.

He ran through empty hallways of the palace, dodging boxes and ladders and tubs. Heaving open the heavy door, he dashed down the long corridor to the closet. Oh, was he thrilled! Setting down the lantern, he performed a victory dance—rather like the soldiers in Virgil!—jabbing the key at mock foes. How clever he'd been. Poor Bramante with his face full of sauce and his mouth full of sweets. He'd have quite a head in the morning.

Even the closet did not scare Federico tonight. He swag-gered over and threw open the door. The eight small mirrors glinted but the closet otherwise stood empty.

With a toss of his head, he swung the door shut. *"These are my final words; I spill them with my blood!"* he declared as the bells of Saint Mary Major faded away. Oh, did the Latin sound glorious when it was properly spoken. *"Rise from my ashes, children, and wreak vengeance!"* He slipped off his cap to polish the glass balls, and jauntily set it back on his curls. Leaping onto a stack of planks, he threw his arms wide. *"No peace on sea, nor on land; battle forever, my sons—"*

"Mrow."

Federico spun, peering down the corridor. Juno trotted toward him, her tail as tall as a banner. "Juno! How'd you get out?"

She leaped onto the stack to join him. "Mrow." All the explanation he'd get, apparently.

"Well, keep me company till Herbert arrives."

She rubbed against his leg. "Mrow," she agreed. *I love you.*

"I love you, too. I've just remembered another verse—do you want to hear? It begins 'Haec ate,' I think."

"Mrow." Juno vaulted off the planks for the closet. Luckily the door was closed.

"Or is it 'Haec ait'?"

She scratched at the closet door.

"Don't do that—"

With a tug of her paw, Juno pulled the door open. He had not latched it properly.

"No!" Federico leaped off the stack.

She slipped inside.

"No—" He hurled himself forward, pulling the door wide. She was gone.

"Juno!" *Don't panic,* he told himself. Soon Santo Spirito would ring, and all the other churches, and Herbert would appear with Juno, just as before. Federico must simply shut the door—properly this time—and wait.

He paced, biting his nails in the thundering silence. The dark night hovered beyond the windows; the heavens gaped down. That dreadful closet. He hated it.

*Bonngg,* began the bells of Santo Spirito. *Bonngg.*

Federico sagged with relief. Now at last his friend would be here. His friend and his cat. His friends. Both of them.

*Bonngg,* the bells continued.

He kept his eyes on the closet door. Light glinted on the eight glass balls. The holly wood inlay glowed palely beside the ebony black. But no click of the latch. No greeting.

No *mrow;* no Juno.

*Bonngg. . . .*

*Bonngg. . . .*

Church after church struck midnight. Santa Maria in Trastevere. San Silvestro. Santa Francesca. Federico waited and waited. But his friends, it seemed, would never return.

# PART II

# NOW, AND THEN

*Chapter 9*

## BEE OF BROOKLYN

Bee slumped against the Subaru window, staring at the trees flashing by. "Why would anyone live here? It's so boring."

"It's not boring. Look, a bicycle." Mom pointed as she drove. "Lots of people live here. I bet some of them are even happy." They passed a man walking a golden retriever. "See? That's nice." She squeezed Bee's knee. "I'm sorry, Queen Bee."

Bee was supposed to be in Italy right now, spending the summer with her grandparents like always. But Nonna and Pepe had won a last-minute cruise, so instead she was stuck with her moms.

Bee crossed her arms over her T-shirt—her favorite T-shirt, black with a gold crown on the front. Probably no one around here wore T-shirts like hers, or black leggings. "He should have gotten a shelter dog."

"Maybe it is a shelter dog. Maybe it's a rescue." Mom pulled into the driveway of a big white house. "Who knows?"

Bee sat up. "Wait—what? Why are we stopping here?"

Mom unbuckled her seatbelt. "Remember that couple Moo helped? They needed someone to house sit. So ta-da."

Bee stared at the house. It had a lawn and flowerpots and green shutters. The front porch even had a swing. "Wow." She'd never seen a porch swing in real life.

"Don't forget to carry stuff in," Mom called as she unlocked the front door.

"I know," Bee sighed. Mom and Moo were always telling her to carry stuff in. She shouldered her book bag, so heavy she could barely make it up the steps. Inside the house were couches and coffee tables and pale blue walls. "This place is wild."

"Don't forget to take your shoes off," Mom called.

"Do I have to?" Bee plopped down on the polished wood floor. "It takes forever."

"You could wear other shoes."

"I don't like other shoes." Moo had bought Bee two pairs of high-tops after Bee begged and pleaded and made a video. It was always a big decision, which combination to wear. The indigo (left) plus violet (right) was her favorite, and Moo's.

"Come on in. I've got hummus and ginger ale."

"Ginger ale?" Bee padded into the kitchen. It was huge and shiny, like in a magazine. "But Moo says soda equals sugar equals poison."

"Well, Moo's not here." Mom grinned at her, looking around the kitchen with a loaf of bread in her hand. "These people weren't rich, you know. But her father was a doctor way back when. The living room used to be his exam room."

Bee dragged a carrot through the hummus. "Are there ghosts?"

"You wish. Anyway, one day the woman was cleaning out a cupboard and found an old drawing. Like, really old. Pen and ink." Mom taught art history. She could talk about ink for hours.

Bee waited, carrot in hand. "And?"

"And it turned out to be by Michelangelo."

"Wait—Michelangelo? *The* Michelangelo?"

"Yep. And they sold it. Guess how much."

"I dunno. A million dollars?"

"Six point five."

"Six point five what? Million?" Bee dropped the carrot. "Six point five million *dollars*?"

"You don't remember Moo talking about this? So they sold it and fixed up the house, and now they're on vacation in Hawaii."

"Wait a minute." Bee retrieved the carrot. "How did a drawing by Michelangelo get into a cupboard in nowhere New Jersey?"

Mom put broccoli in the fridge. "They think the doctor got it as payment back in the forties. So much art was being smuggled out of Europe during World War II—"

"It was stolen?" Why hadn't anyone told Bee this story?

"No one could prove it. Moo was one of the specialists they brought in."

Bee peered around the kitchen. "Maybe there are a couple more hidden somewhere."

"Don't even think about it. You're on your best behavior, understand? These people are being very nice about letting us stay here."

"I'm always on my best behavior."

Mom's cell phone rang. "Hey there," she said, putting it on speaker. "How'd the meeting go?"

"Un tempo sprecato." *A waste of time.* Moo always switched to Italian when she was mad. "I'm already at the train station. Hey, Bombo, you like the house?"

"It's great. Especially the water." Bee took a gulp of ginger ale, grinning at Mom. Mom grinned back.

"You take your shoes off inside, okay? And you do not climb the trees."

"It was only one tree and it wasn't that high."

"You gave me a heart attack," Moo scolded.

*She's Italian,* Mom mouthed, shrugging at Bee. "Moo, as fascinating as this conversation is, I've got a speech in three hours." Mom was going to a conference—that's why they were in New Jersey. "I'm still thinking about changing the last picture. . . ."

Bee skittered out of the kitchen. She'd been listening to speech talk for months. "I'll be outside."

"Hey, Bombo," Moo called, "tonight we make pizza, maybe?"

"Yes!" Bee punched the air. "You're the best, Moo." She

bounded out, settling on the swing to lace her high-tops. A porch swing—how cool was that? She could spend all day out here, drinking ginger ale and reading every book in her bag. She grinned, rocking. She should send a picture to Nonna and Pepe. And tonight was homemade pizza!

She leaned back to look at the house. Why green shutters? If she owned this place, she'd paint the shutters pink or orange—one of Michelangelo's colors. That was a pretty amazing story. Imagine going through a cupboard and finding a drawing worth millions of dollars. That was fun art history. Not Mom's kind about speeches and ink.

She studied the house. Not orange shutters, she decided. Maybe violet, like her high-tops. You never saw purple on houses even though it was such a great color—

A crash jolted her upright. "Peep peep peep peep!" A bird was in trouble, somewhere close, off to Bee's right.

Slowly she crept toward the sound: off the porch, past a shrub, into the yard next door and a tangle of tall grass. . . .

A cat hunched under a bush, a fluttering sparrow in its jaws. "Hey," Bee cried, batting aside the branches. The cat glared at her and leaped away. But Bee leaped, too—she didn't play kickball for nothing—and caught the cat's tail.

"Let it go!" Off the bird flew in a blur.

The cat spun and scratched at her, but Bee knew a thing or two about cats. Pepe had barn cats that were meaner than snakes. She'd spent whole summers keeping them away from the chickens. She gripped the cat. "You shouldn't even be outside. Do you know how many songbirds get killed every year by house cats? Three billion." Bee had done a report on it. Cat owners never thought about birds.

The cat glared at her. Its fur was yellow like a lion, and its eyes were yellow, too, with black edges. Kind of Goth, or Ancient Egyptian. At least it was no longer scratching.

Bee backtracked across the yard and banged open the front door. The cat hunkered in her arms, whining a low growl.

Mom sat in the living room with her laptop, phone to her ear. "I'm just not sure that's a strong enough visual. . . ." She flapped her hand at Bee. "What are you doing?" she whispered. "That's not our cat. What, Moo? I missed the rest of that."

Bee glared down at the cat hanging like a sack. "But it was killing birds."

"Take it outside! How about this one?" Mom asked, tapping her laptop.

The cat stared up at Bee. "Mrow?"

"Don't try to charm me." Bee stomped out the door. She couldn't just let it go. This cat's owner needed to learn how dangerous cats were to the environment.

She marched toward the neighbor's house, her jaw set.

She almost lost her nerve. The place next door didn't look like a picture in a magazine—more like an illustration in a book. A scary book. The grass was higher than Bee's shins. Paint peeled off the shutters. "I'm doing this to save lives," she hissed as she rang the doorbell.

"Mrow," the cat grumbled.

"It's your own fault." Bee rang the doorbell again.

"I'm coming," a voice warbled. The lock clicked. "May I help you?" An old woman held the door with one bony hand. She gripped a cane with the other.

"I'm sorry to interrupt," Bee began, "but house cats kill three billion songbirds a year—"

The old woman stared at the cat. "Juno?" she whispered.

"Three billion," Bee repeated. Maybe she had the wrong house? "Cats kill for fun, not because they need to eat—"

"Is it really you?" The woman reached toward the cat. "All those years he hoped you'd return. . . ." She looked up at

Bee and screamed. "*Tu!*" she cried in Italian. *You!* Her hand shot out.

Bee jerked back. The cat bolted out of her arms.

"Cosa stai facendo qui?" The old woman clutched Bee's T-shirt. *What are you doing here?* And then, in English: "How did you get out?"

*Chapter 10*

## MISS BOTHER'S FRIEND

Bee clung to Mom. "It was scary!" She hadn't cried like this in years.

Mom rubbed Bee's back. "It sounds terrible."

"She just kept yelling in Italian. And then she started coughing, and all I could think of was Nonna and Pepe."

"Don't worry, Queen Bee. They're both strong as bulls."

"Let's go back to Brooklyn right now. I'll grab the ginger ale and you get your laptop—"

"Oh, dear."

Bee looked up. They were on the couch, with Mom's stuff all over the coffee table. Through the window Bee could see the old lady tapping her way up the front walk. "Run!" Bee cried.

"Shh. Besides, we won't have to run very fast."

The doorbell rang.

Mom stood, giving Bee a pat. "I'm sure there's an explanation."

"Yeah: we shouldn't have come here." Bee pressed herself against the living-room wall, listening to snatches of conversation: *So dreadfully sorry* and *I did not mean. . . .* And Mom saying it was okay and that she understood and that she'd be delighted.

The door shut. Mom returned to the living room. "What do you know? We're invited to tea."

Bee flopped onto the couch. "Are you crazy?"

Mom laughed. "Apparently you gave her quite a shock."

"She gave me a shock. Seriously, it was horrible—"

"You look like a friend she had when she was a girl. And the cat looked like a pet of her father's. . . . Ready?"

"Wait—now?"

"She's already put on the kettle. I said I have a speech tonight but she was pretty insistent. It'll only be for a few minutes."

Bee crossed her arms. "I'm not going."

"Suit yourself. But who knows? You might find Miss Bother interesting."

"Miss what?" That was a weird name.

"Miss Bother. Her father was a big art dealer back in the day." Mom grabbed her purse. "They say he's the one who gave the Michelangelo drawing to the doctor. That's what Moo told me, anyway."

"They say? Why don't they just ask Miss whatever her name is?"

Mom cocked an eyebrow at Bee. "Miss Bother. She refuses to answer."

And so Bee found herself in Miss Bother's living room, on a lumpy couch that smelled of mothballs and oldness. Paintings signed H BOTHER hung on the walls. A little table held an old-fashioned phone with a twisty cord.

Miss Bother offered a plate that shook in her grip. "A cookie?" Her voice was so old that it quavered.

"Thank you." The cookie crumbled in Bee's hand. The teacup looked held together by stains. "Did your father paint those pictures?"

"Oh, yes. He loved art, my father. He loved to make it,

he loved to collect it, he loved to share it. Especially the art of Italy. We spent much time there."

"*Me, too,*" said Bee—in Italian, to demonstrate. "*I live there every summer.*"

"*What a gift. My father insisted I maintain my Italian.*" Miss Bother turned to Mom. "Do you speak it?" she asked in English.

Mom put down her teacup. "Lucky Bee is fluent, but I'm still learning."

Bee studied the paintings. They were kind of sweet, like kindergarten artwork on a fridge. She didn't see anything worth millions of dollars. "Did your dad," she said, trying to sound casual, "you know, ever own a Michelangelo?"

Mom shot her a glare, but Miss Bother only smiled. "My father found art in odd places. Many of his stories I myself don't believe." She took a sip, staring out the window. "Sometimes he'd recommend the buyer hold onto the piece for a while. Let the questions fade."

"So he actually did have that Michelangelo drawing?" Bee was being rude; she knew that. But she really wanted to know.

Miss Bother gazed at Bee, her eyes bright. "We have

not been acquainted long, young lady. But I believe you are capable of solving any puzzle." She turned to Mom. "You are visiting the university?"

Mom gave Bee a warning look. "I'm speaking at a conference tonight, in fact."

Bee peered at the photographs on the side table: a girl and a man on horseback somewhere out west. The two of them in front of the Eiffel Tower. In a gondola in Venice.

"My father and I," Miss Bother explained. "He adopted me when I was ten. He promised he'd never leave me, and he never did till the day he died." She waved a bony arm at sketches of a kitten. "And that is Juno. He always hoped she would come back. He made special accommodations."

Bee scanned the photos. "Where's your mom?"

"Bee!" Mom hissed. Mom could hiss anything. But Bee got questions all the time about her dad and where her dad was and who was her dad.

"I'm afraid I have no memories of my mother. But my father made the two of us a family. He saved my life, you know. I had diphtheria, and he rushed me to the doctor—the doctor who owned the house you're in now." She pulled down her collar. "Do you see this scar? The doctor had to make a hole so I could breathe. That's how swollen my throat was."

"That's horrible." Bee was absolutely doing her next science report on diphtheria.

"It was. . . ." Miss Bother's voice trailed off. "Forgive me. I must confess I invited you here for a reason." She struggled to stand, and Mom jumped to help. "You're too kind." She tapped into the dining room, to a painting of a peacock hanging over the fireplace. It might have been a peacock. It had H BOTHER at the bottom. "If you could"—she nodded to Mom—"there is a latch on the left side. Pull the frame, please."

Mom felt for the latch, and the picture swung out from the wall. Bee gasped in delight. She adored secret hiding places! There was another picture behind it. A drawing.

"I'm afraid I can't reach it anymore. It's so nice you're here—I haven't seen my friend in years."

Mom stumbled backward. "Bee, it's you."

Bee's jaw dropped. She was looking at a drawing of herself. A drawing of Bee with shoulder-length curls. The girl even had the scar from the can opener, and a mole. "It's me."

Miss Bother nodded. "Now you can understand my surprise."

"But—" Mom struggled. "I've never seen this before. Have you?"

Bee shook her head. No way. The girl in the drawing looked so sad!

"The pen work is stunning—it looks sixteenth century," Mom said. "Oh, and *Undici anni*. . . . What's that? 'The age to say?'"

"It means eleven years," said Bee. Mom's Italian was so bad. "Hey, just like me."

"Her birthday was last month," Mom explained to Miss Bother.

"Well, happy birthday, Beatrice." She pronounced Bee's name the Italian way, with the extra chiming syllable. "I must get you a gift."

"That's okay." Bee didn't want anything, except maybe this drawing. The drawing was super cool. "It's so beautiful." Not that she *wanted* it. But. "Moo will totally flip over this."

Miss Bother sighed. "You have heard, I am sure, about my neighbors? So many years they spent getting their treasure approved. How lucky they were that Michelangelo took the time to sign his sketch." She glanced around at the sagging drapes, the worn carpet, the paint peeling from the ceiling. "I am very happy for them."

"Wait, did Michelangelo do this? He didn't draw girls." Even Bee knew that.

"Certainly not. But I know who did." Miss Bother eased herself into a chair. "There is disagreement, however. So much disagreement that it cannot be sold."

Mom couldn't take her eyes off the drawing. "Maybe someone saw you online? I mean, it's *you*, Bee. How long have you had this, Miss Bother?"

"Much longer than computers." Miss Bother chuckled. "My father found it in Italy even before he found me."

Mom looked skeptical. "So who do you think drew it?"

"You're a scholar." Miss Bother smiled. "I'm sure you've seen his work elsewhere."

"Maybe," offered Bee. It did look kind of familiar. But she'd seen thousands—seriously, *thousands*—of pictures. She spent half her life in museums.

"Oh, you have." Miss Bother looked from Bee to Mom, and back to Bee. "You know him well, I suspect. The great Renaissance master. Raphael."

## *Chapter 11*
## THE SIGN

Mom was way more upset than Bee. From the moment they left Miss Bother's house—Miss Bother promising that Beatrice could come back anytime—Mom was spinning. She sat scrolling through her laptop, twisting her lip between her fingers. "It doesn't make any sense."

"You're going to end up looking like Jabba the Hutt if you keep doing that," Bee warned her.

"Even if the drawing was by someone very talented, who knows you, of all people—"

"What's so bad about me?"

"You know what I mean. And how would they know to

hide it there? Even we didn't know you'd be here until four days ago." She shook her head. "That darn cruise."

"Maybe they got my photo from school. Hey, maybe I have a secret twin! Do I have a secret twin? How come you never told me? Mom?"

But Mom was already on the phone with Moo. She disappeared into the other room, whispering.

Why did they need to whisper? It was just a drawing that happened to look exactly like Bee and also happened to be in a secret hiding place in a mysterious old house which made it the coolest thing in the history of ever. Miss Bother had said to come back anytime. What did that mean, exactly? How many minutes should Bee wait? She should bring something. Cookies, maybe. Miss Bother certainly needed better cookies.

Mom returned, pocketing her phone. "Moo agrees it's very strange. She's curious about Miss Bother's dialect. You know, every region of Italy has its own way of talking. How did she sound to you?"

"I don't know. Upset? Hey, can I bake cookies? Because I would be super-clean. I promise."

Mom, still twisting her lip, joined Bee at the window

to stare at Miss Bother's. "I wish I didn't have this speech tonight."

"I'll clean the whole kitchen before Moo gets here. Even the pans."

"I just don't know what it means." Mom's phone rang. "Hey, what's up?"

Maybe Bee had a secret admirer from the year 1500. Maybe it was a sign, like in a book.

"You're kidding." Mom rubbed her forehead. "Well, tell them to hurry up and fix it. . . . Yeah." She hung up. "Moo's train is delayed. So you'll have to come with me till she gets in."

Bee collapsed onto the couch. "Mom, no! I'll be the only kid. Or there'll be one kid who's Russian and who spends every minute gaming."

"Maybe I could find a sitter."

"A sitter?" Bee was outraged. "You leave me alone all the time."

"I leave you sometimes, in our very safe apartment." She gestured at Miss Bother's house. "But with that—"

"Mom." Bee stopped her. "Remember in *When You Reach Me*, when Miranda gets those messages that turn out to be from the future?"

Mom made a face. "So that drawing is telling us the world is going to end and I'm going to win $20,000." Mom also liked *When You Reach Me.*

"Or the lamppost in *The Magician's Nephew,* the one Lucy finds in *The Lion, the Witch and the Wardrobe?*"

"The drawing is a portal to Narnia. Why didn't I think of that?"

"It's—" But Bee couldn't say that it was only a sign. That would freak Mom out even more. She pulled her tattered copy of *The Lion, the Witch and the Wardrobe* out of her bag. "Look. I'll just sit on the couch reading until Moo gets here. I won't even start the cookies."

Somehow—Bee couldn't quite believe it—Mom agreed. After talking to Moo again, and figuring out Bee would only be alone for twenty minutes, and checking that Bee knew how use the house phone because she still didn't have a cell even though this was a perfect example of why she needed one. . . .

Finally, Mom drove off with her laptop and bag and scarf (indigo!) that she'd bought especially for the speech. The scarf was the same color as the sky outside, actually—the top of the sky. The rest of the sky was still sunset.

Bee plopped onto the couch. Even from the couch she

could see Miss Bother's house, and a light in Miss Bother's living room, and fireflies in the yard. There was still time for cookies. Moo would love the drawing, too.

She flipped through *The Lion, the Witch and the Wardrobe*. Lucy's parents never talked about babysitters. Lucy's parents weren't even around. Lucy got to ride lions.

Bee snuck another look at Miss Bother's. Wait—what? There was something in the yard . . . a cat. The yellow cat with black-lined eyes.

"Don't you dare," Bee whispered as the cat slunk through the grass.

The cat leaped, and Bee gasped—

But the cat was only batting at fireflies.

Bee snorted. "Joke's on you." Fireflies were super bitter. That's how they got away with being so obvious. One bite of firefly and you never wanted more.

Bored with fireflies, the cat wandered toward Miss Bother's house. She climbed the kitchen steps, blurry in the shadows— and suddenly she was no longer there. She had vanished.

Bee grabbed the phone, punching in numbers. "Answer, answer," she whispered.

"What's up, Queen Bee?" Mom sounded like she was in

a room full of people. Which, hello, she was.

"Mom, listen. That yellow cat? It just, like, vaporized."

"Water, please," Mom said to someone. "Bee, I'm kind of in the middle of something. You're being ridiculous."

"Oh. Right. Sorry." Quickly Bee dialed Moo.

"Pronto, Bombo, come stai?" *Hey, Bumblebee, how are you?* *Bombo* was Italian for "hornet," mostly, but it could also mean "bumblebee." Bee and Moo preferred bumblebee.

"I'm okay but there's this cat in the yard that just, like, vaporized. . . ."

"You are not bringing a cat into the house again?"

"No. But it's really strange." She glanced over at Miss Bother's house. A light flickered in the living room, but that was it.

"We'll take a look when I get there, okay? Now you stay safe like a little bee and do not move. I am bringing your favorite mozzarella. Ciao bella." *Bye, gorgeous.*

Bee set down the phone and took another glance. There— the cat! Sitting on the back steps licking a paw.

Bee squinted. It must have come through the kitchen door somehow. . . .

The cat vanished back into the house.

Bee pressed her face to the window. It sure was hard to see through the twilight and the overgrown bushes, and the flickering lamp didn't help. What had Miss Bother said? Something about her father making accommodations for a cat.

As Bee watched, the cat's head appeared.

Bee sagged in disappointment. The kitchen had a cat door, duh. Now that she looked, she could see it clearly. There was a flap and everything.

The cat threaded its way through the shaggy lawn. Flicker flicker flicker, went the soft yellow light from Miss Bother's house. Then longer flickers, like fliiicker fliiicker. Or maybe flowker. . . . How would you describe a long flicker? Then flicker flicker flicker again.

That was weird.

Flicker flicker flicker stop. Flowker flowker flowker stop. Flicker flicker flicker. Three flickers, three flowkers, three flickers—

"Wait—what?" Bee leaped to her feet. "It's SOS!" With trembling fingers, she dialed Moo. "Moo, she's calling SOS."

"Who? This train, I could push it faster."

"The old lady next door. The light is blinking SOS."

Moo's voice rose. "Where is this SOS? Are you safe?"

"Yes, I'm safe," Bee sighed. "It's the lady next door with the Raphael drawing."

"Possibly Raphael. There is no signature."

"It's an SOS," Bee repeated. "What do I do?"

"You stay there, you lock the door, you do not talk to anyone. Capisce?" *Understand?* "I will be there in half an hour, it looks like. Questo stupido treno." *This stupid train.* "Sit tightly. Ciao."

"Ciao." Bee frowned at the phone. Half an hour was forever. What if something was really wrong? What if something had happened to Miss Bother? She couldn't just sit tightly. She needed to act.

*Chapter 12*

## YOU'LL MAKE EVERYTHING BETTER

"Miss Bother?" Bee rang the doorbell, listening to it echo. "Miss Bother?"

"Beatrice?" came a weak cry. "Sei tu?" *Is that you?*

Bee put her mouth to the door. "Miss Bother, it's Bee." Although Miss Bother knew that already. "Is everything okay?"

"Hello, Beatrice," Miss Bother called in her quavery old voice. "I'm afraid I've had a bit of a spill."

See? Something was wrong. Bee had been super smart to run over. "Miss Bother, I'm going to come in, okay? I'm opening the door now."

"Mrow."

Bee jumped, startled, as the cat padded across the porch. "Dumb cat," she muttered under her breath. "Um, Miss Bother, the door is locked."

The cat pawed at the door. "Mrow," it ordered.

"It's locked, you dummy."

Miss Bother's voice trickled through the wood. "I'm afraid I can't reach it. Oh dear . . ."

"Mrow." The cat stalked away, tail lashing.

"Thanks a lot," Bee called. "You could chip in, you know." Bee was always being told to chip in— *That was it!* She raced after the cat. "Hey, wait up."

By the time she reached the back of the house, the cat was nowhere to be seen. But there: the cat door. Bee knelt on the steps. "Miss Bother?"

"Goodness me, Beatrice, where are you?" Miss Bother's voice was much clearer.

"I'm at the cat door."

"Goodness, how remarkable."

"I know, right?" The cat door was pretty big, actually. Big enough for her shoulders. If Bee stretched one arm and twisted . . .

"Are you hurt?" Miss Bother sounded worried.

"I'm okay," Bee grunted. She wriggled her hips, pulling her knees through. . . . She was in.

She stood up, brushing at her T-shirt and leggings. The kitchen smelled of fish, eww. A tuna sandwich sat on the counter next to dirty cups. Bee hated the smell of tuna fish.

"Goodness me, if I'd known the cat door was so accessible—"

"Don't worry." Bee peered around the living room, looking for Miss Bother. "I can wiggle out of anything. That's what my grandpa Pepe says." She stepped into the front hall. "Miss Bother! Are you okay?"

Miss Bother was lying across the stairs, still holding her cane. She smiled up at Bee. "Beatrice. Che bella." *How beautiful.* "It gives me such pleasure to finally know your name."

Bee tried to think of something to say besides *Are you okay?* "Um, I saw your SOS."

"Aren't you clever?" With great effort, Miss Bother stretched out her cane to push the light switch. "I could just reach it." She lay back with a wince. "For so long I've hoped you would come."

"I'm really sorry. I should have figured out the SOS right away."

"Poor Beatrice, that's not what I meant. Goodness, your shoes are two different colors."

"I've got another pair just like them at home." No matter how many times she said it, the joke never got old.

"Oh, it hurts to laugh. I wish I had shoes like that when I was a girl."

"You should get some now."

"Can you imagine?" Miss Bother beamed up at her. "The girl from Raphael. And here you are at last—"

A crash startled them both—the crack of breaking china. Miss Bother winced in pain.

The cat trotted into the living room carrying the tuna sandwich. "Mrow," it whined, kind of muffled, dropping it with a look of disgust.

"*Juno!*" cried Miss Bother. "Look, Beatrice. It's Juno."

"You mean your father's old cat?" It was so embarrassing, having to ask.

Miss Bother didn't seem embarrassed, though. "He always said she'd return. Come, Juno."

The cat sniffed at the sandwich, ignoring them.

Bee squirmed, trying to figure out where to look. Maybe Miss Bother had hit her head. Or maybe she was a little, you know, the way old people got. The way Grandpa Pepe always lost his glasses. "I, um, I think I should call Moo."

"Here, Juno—Moo? Who is that?"

"It's what I call my mom. She calls me Bombo."

"Oh, that's marvelous. A wild little bee!"

Bee grinned. "She named me that when I first starting walking. I don't know why."

"You must have been quite a bundle of energy." Miss Bother smiled, her head resting on a step. "And now you are here with your portrait."

Bee glanced toward the dining room. The drawing wasn't Bee, obviously. But still, it was interesting. Like a sign . . .

Giving the tuna a last dismissive sniff, the cat wandered away.

"Don't go, Juno." Miss Bother tried to shift and grimaced. "Oh dear, I truly am hurt. Beatrice, mi amore"—*my love*— "might you call me an ambulance?"

Bee straightened. "Really?" She'd never called an ambulance before.

Miss Bother waved toward the living room. "There's the phone."

It wasn't easy, though. Bee had never used an old-fashioned phone. "How do you—oh." She stared at the circular part that went round and round. "That's why people say *dial*." Finally she reached 911, and answered all their questions, and put the handle thing back on its base. "Someone's on the way. . . . Hey, that's why you say *hang up!* Because you hang the phone up. Wow." All these terms that had never made sense.

Miss Bother lay back, closing her eyes. "I must confess, Beatrice, that I had quite lost hope."

"I'm so sorry—it's just that I've never used this kind of phone—"

"Come, Beatrice. I must tell you something." With effort, Miss Bother reached for Bee's hand. Her skin was so thin that blue veins showed through. Bee had to sit close to hear her. "My father found your drawing in Italy, in a little city—"

"Um," Bee interrupted, "the drawing isn't really me." Just to be clear.

Miss Bother smiled. "It did not have Raphael's signature, however. So my father traveled to Rome—back to Rome—to acquire it."

"You mean like a forgery?" Bee knew that word from Moo. It meant fake.

"Quite the opposite. While in Rome, however, he found me. He never returned there. What if something happened, and I was left alone? But it made him very sad." She squeezed Bee's hand. "You'll fix it, won't you?"

"Um, sure. Can I, um, get you some water?" She hoped the ambulance got here soon. There was definitely a problem with Miss Bother's head.

"I wish you could have met him. He was so wonderful." Miss Bother twisted, straining to look up the stairs. "I haven't been inside his office in years—I never wanted to see it again. Not until today."

Red and blue lights flashed through the window. Whew.

"Excuse me." Gently Bee pulled her hand away. "I, um, need to get the door."

Heavy footsteps crossed the porch. "EMTs," a man shouted.

"Beatrice?"

"Yes, Miss Bother?" Bee paused, her hand on the knob.

"I know you can do this."

And then the house was filled with emergency medical technicians and their rolling bed and their loud, loud voices. Loudly—like Miss Bother was deaf—they asked about her medicines and her age, checking her temp and blood pressure, writing everything down.

The EMTs acted super professional, but Bee could see them looking at the chipping paint, the dust-covered mirror, the stained rugs. *It's not her fault,* she wanted to say. *It's not her fault she's old.*

"So you were going up the stairs when you fell?" the guy EMT asked, shooting a sideways glance at the tuna sandwich on the floor.

"Yes. I had just received word from an old friend." Miss Bother looked right at Bee when she said this.

"So who's next of kin?" the woman EMT asked Bee. The EMT's hair was pulled back in one of those tight buns Bee could never make.

"Um, we're just staying next door. We got here today." *We would have helped if we'd known!*

"This young woman was simply—helping," Miss Bother whispered. She gasped as they lifted her onto the bed-thing and strapped her in. "She's going—to fix it—"

"Let's get you to the hospital," the guy said, pushing the bed.

"Bye, Miss Bother." Bee did her best to sound cheerful as Miss Bother rolled by. She looked so small, lying there! Like she was disappearing. "You're going to be fine."

"Thank you for coming, Beatrice." Miss Bother's voice was almost lost in the commotion, her face creased with pain. Even so, she smiled. "I know you'll make everything better."

## Chapter 13
## ALONE IN THE HOUSE

Bee watched the EMTs slide Miss Bother into the ambulance and drive off. Then she raced back to the living room to call Mom.

She shouldn't call Mom; she knew that. Mom was right in the middle of a huge speech. But Bee suspected Moo would not be one hundred percent happy with what had just happened. She'd say *I told you to sit tightly.* She'd say *you go into a strange house through the cat door?* So instead Bee dialed Mom. Well, Mom's voicemail. "You've reached Miriam Bliss," the voice said. "Please leave a message."

"Hi, Mom. I hope your speech is good, everything's great

here. I um—" Should she mention crawling into Miss Bother's kitchen and calling an ambulance? Hard to sum that up. "Just letting you know I'm okay and I'll be home soon—I mean, home is great. I'm here now. Bye." She hung up the phone before she said anything worse. Why did she have to mention the home thing?

Now she was going to have to call Moo. She sighed, picking up the phone—

And stepped on the tuna fish sandwich.

"Eww!" The tuna squished up the sides of her high-top, almost touching the fabric. "That's so gross!" She glared around the living room but of course the cat was gone. Cats always skipped out on trouble.

Holding her nose, Bee hopped into the kitchen and jammed her leg into the sink. She *hated* the smell of tuna fish. "This is my favorite shoe, you dumb cat," she muttered, scrubbing the violet fabric. Bits of soggy bread stuck to the dishes in the sink. Yuck. She stomped back into the living room. "Dumb cat," she repeated.

Her eyes drifted toward the dining room. The peacock painting.

She needed to call Moo. She should go home and call Moo

from there. And she would, right away. But first she needed one more look at the drawing. Her drawing. Her Raphael. Five minutes: that's all. She deserved it, really, because of the tuna fish.

She crossed the hall, watching where she stepped just in case, and flicked on the dining room lights. The table had a pile of envelopes with words like URGENT and OPEN IMMEDIATELY. One end of the room had a brown folding screen. The curtains hung heavy with dust.

Quick as she could, Bee dragged a chair to the fireplace and climbed up, feeling for the latch. The peacock painting swung out. . . .

And there it was. A sketch more than a drawing, of a girl with dark curls and a face full of sadness.

Bee leaned in, studying it. She touched the scar on her own cheek. Thanks to the scar, she now knew the Italian word for *can opener*—l'apriscatole—and for *stitches*—suture. The girl in the drawing had curly hair the same length as hers. And a mole under her eye, and a small scratch on her neck. . . .

Wait—Bee had a scratch on her neck?

Carefully she climbed off the chair, heading for the mirror beside the front door. Yup, there it was: a scratch from climbing the tree. She hadn't even noticed. It was almost healed, but not quite.

It was like the drawing had been made of her *today.*

She stared at herself in the dim light. Mom had straight hair that always looked like a haircut, but Bee and Moo both had nothing but curls. Everyone thought Bee came from Moo because of the hair. Sometimes Mom found it funny. Sometimes she didn't.

Bee marched back to the dining room and onto the chair. The girl's hair was, like, *exactly* the same. "What is going on?" she murmured. "Where did he find you?"

"Mrow."

Bee jerked in fright, grabbing the mantel just in time.

The yellow cat stood in the doorway, tail waving.

"You almost killed me*!*"

The cat wandered to the far end of the dining room, behind the folding screen painted with roses and pigeons brown with age.

Bee crawled off the chair. "Get out of here*!*" She stomped after the cat. "Wait, what?"

Behind the screen was a bed—a narrow little bed with a creased pillow and rumpled sheets. This was where Miss

Bother slept? A huge house, and she slept here?

Oh. Oh, wow. Miss Bother slept in the dining room. She couldn't climb the stairs. That's why she fell. Because she hadn't climbed in so long, and then she tried.

Bee felt sick. This was really, really wrong. Didn't Miss Bother have a family? Didn't she have someone to help her?

"Mrow," the cat called from the hall.

"Hey! You. Juno." Although it couldn't be Juno, because that was Miss Bother's father's cat from a million years ago. "You shouldn't be here," Bee said crossly. "*We* shouldn't be here." Her five minutes were over.

"Mrow." The cat trotted up the stairs.

"Oh no, you don't. This isn't your house." The stairs were so dusty that Bee could see the cat's paw prints. Footprints, too, on the first couple of steps—hers and Miss Bother's. Then one step with a handprint and a smudge.

That's where Miss Bother had fallen. Bee stared at it, skin prickling. Miss Bother hadn't used these stairs for years, maybe. And then she'd decided to climb them today. . . .

"Mrow," the cat called from the landing.

Why today? Because the cat was here? Because Bee was? Because of the drawing?

"Mrow." Maybe the cat was trying to tell her something. Show her. Maybe—just maybe—it was a sign.

Bee couldn't stop. Not now.

Up she climbed after the cat, to the second floor and a bedroom with a dark wood bed. "Cat?" The dresser had a man's watch and a pen lying out like a display in a museum. A painting hung above the dresser, an H BOTHER painting of a hospital bed and a girl who looked very sick. But the hospital table held a bouquet of flowers, and the girl's quilt was full of color.

"Miss Bother," Bee breathed.

"Mrow. . . ."

Oh, right. The cat. Bee followed the noise through the bedroom into a bathroom with a yellowed claw-foot tub. The cat stood on the edge of the sink, batting the faucet. "Mrow."

"What is it? Oh. You're thirsty." With effort, Bee turned on the water.

The cat cocked its head, lapping away. "Mrow," it mumbled. Possibly *Thank you.* Possibly.

A toothbrush lay neatly on the sink next to a rusty white and red can—another museum display. "Colgate Tooth Powder," Bee read out loud. "How cool is that? People used to brush their teeth with powder."

The cat trotted away.

Bee turned off the faucet. "Hey, wait up." By the time she made it out of the bedroom, the cat was halfway to the third floor.

Bee paused. She really didn't think she should be here. But—

"Mrow."

"Okay." She flicked on the staircase lights. "I hope you know what you're doing."

The third floor was seriously creepy—an attic, really, more than a floor. A tarnished chandelier barely lit the sloping ceiling. One wall held a built-in bookcase iced with dust. A low door was tucked under the eaves.

"Juno?" Bee didn't like that low dark door. It looked like a little cage.

But no *mrow*. No pad of paws. The house stood silent.

Bee eased her way to the bookcase. It had a whole shelf of *Art Bulletin*, and another shelf of books with tattered yellow covers.

"Look at that!" Bee whispered, tickled in spite of herself. "Nancy Drew." She loved Nancy Drew. Nancy Drew would be a pretty good buddy right now. "Hey, cat, where are you?"

What would Nancy Drew do? Bee needed to think like a detective.

She dropped to her hands and knees, peering across the dust. There: a trail of paw prints leading from the stairs to the bookcase . . . and *into* the bookcase. Like the cat just vanished.

Bee smacked her forehead. The bookcase must have a secret opening! Nancy Drew would have figured it out right away. In fact, Bee could see a space on the bottom shelf, between two books, with a hole behind it. She could hear an echoing *mrow.*

"This is so cool. Thank you, cat." She poked at the shelves, feeling for a latch. She pulled out the books where a doorknob should be. Nothing.

There were, like, hundreds of books. Italian poetry. Guidebooks. Titles like *A Morning Glory in the Thorns* and *The Lives of the Artists*—

Huh. *The Lives of the Artists.* That seemed like the kind of book Moo and Mom would read . . . or Miss Bother's father.

Bee eased the book from its shelf.

A click. The bookcase swung in.

## Chapter 14
## THE OFFICE

Bee peered into the dark space. Two yellow eyes glowed back. . . .

"Mrow."

The cat. "That's funny," Bee said, in case anyone thought she'd been scared. She felt the wall for a switch. There had to be a switch, right? And there it was, whew.

The light revealed a room with just enough space for a desk and a huge wooden crate. Dust and cobwebs covered everything: the desk, an old phone, a calendar pinned to the wall. Bee could barely read the date: June 1942. "This is incredible," she whispered.

"Mrow," the cat agreed, curling around her ankles.

And the crate: wow. It was covered with weird decorations and even had a door, kind of. But when Bee opened it, there was nothing inside.

She turned to the desk. A picture hung above it, one of those old engravings of a guy with a puffy coat and a beard. In the center of the desk sat the thickest book Bee had ever seen. Dusty bookmarks poked out of the pages. With trembling hands, she wiped off the dust. "This is it, cat. This is it." She sounded out the title, doing her best with the fancy lettering: "Enn Sick Lope—no, En Cy Clo. . . . Oh." Her shoulders dropped. "Encyclopedia." She'd thought it was a book of magic.

The cat jumped onto the desk, leaving a trail of paw prints. "Mrow?"

The cat was right. The book still might be interesting. With effort, Bee opened to a bookmark. The page began with MANTA and ended with MAORI. The entry for MANTUA had been circled.

"Mrow?"

"I don't know Mantua. Do you?" She flipped to another bookmark: MICHELANGELO. "Hey, I know that one." Everyone knew Michelangelo. She turned to a third: GONZAGA. Whatever.

"Mrow." The cat jumped off the desk.

"You said it." Bee pushed the book away. "Can you imagine having to use that to look stuff up? It'd take forever." The internet was so much better.

She peered at yellowed note cards pinned over the desk, each thumbtack with a halo of rust. NO TIME PASSES, one said. Another asked HOW DOES THE CAT MOVE?

Bee laughed. "With its legs, duh." There were drawings, too—arrows bouncing off walls and water, a cube-thing. . . .

"Mrow." The cat pawed at the crate, trying to open the door.

"I already looked. Nothing there." Bee opened the desk drawer—a squeaky metal drawer to match the old metal desk. It was filled with candy in little wrapped parcels. "Hey, look. 'Choco-nutties.'" Bee felt like an archeologist. A candy archeologist, finding ancient candy!

She shook a package. A stream of dead flies fell out. Hastily she slammed the drawer shut, scrubbing her hands on her leggings. "Eww."

"Mrow," the cat insisted.

"I told you, there's nothing in there." She opened the door of the crate: "See? Nothing."

"Mrow," the cat agreed.

Now that Bee thought about it, the crate was pretty weird. It was taller than she was, for one thing. It looked kind of like an antique, with those symbols and a fancy black latch. The door had balls of glass built right into the wood.

Again she peered inside. The back wall had eight small mirrors. And inside the door, kind of pinned to the wood, was a larger glass ball, this one with liquid sealed inside it. "Weird."

"Mrow."

Bee turned back to the note cards. There: mirrors, water, arrows. Wait—those weren't arrows. They were rays of light. She raced back to check the crate. Light definitely went through the glass balls. "Look at that."

The cat stretched, yawning so hard that it squeaked.

Bee frowned at the crate. Why was it here? With some caution this time, she opened the door. Nothing inside except the mirrors and that weird thing of water.

The crate didn't have a rod for hangers. It didn't even have hooks.

It didn't, for example, hold a bunch of fur coats. . . .

But still, Bee knew. This wasn't a crate. It was a wardrobe, in the secret room of a crazy old house. "Narnia!" she gasped. "It's the wardrobe to Narnia." She stared at it, her mind spinning. All her life she'd dreamed of Narnia. What if she could meet Aslan and Mr. Tumnus? What if she saw Lucy?

The cat swiped at the spirally phone cord dangling off the desk. "Mrow—tch!"

"That's really dusty," Bee pointed out. "No wonder you're sneezing." The phone itself was so covered in dust that she couldn't read the numbers in the holes.

The phone. . . .

Oh, no—Bee hadn't called Moo! How long had it been? Maybe Moo was still on the train. "Please don't be mad," Bee begged. Scrunching up her face, she blew the dust off the phone. "Seven . . . one . . . eight," she dialed.

The cat wandered back to the crate-thing, patting the door. "Mrow."

Bee paused, her finger in the 6 MNO hole. She glanced at the staircase, visible through the half-open bookcase, and back at the crate. "It's a wardrobe. It has to be."

"Mrow." It was like the cat was saying *Of course it is. You need to try it.*

Bee hung up the phone. "You're right. I should at least try." She wiped her hands on her T-shirt. Two seconds. That's all it would take. It wouldn't work, but still, she had to try. Then she'd call Moo and tell her the whole story, and they'd make cookies together, and pizza with fresh mozzarella.

She opened the wardrobe door, making the water slosh in that weird glass globe. The eight mirrors gleamed dimly. "Coming?" she asked the cat.

The cat settled back on its haunches. "Mrow."

"Suit yourself." With a deep breath, she stepped inside.

She pulled the door shut.

She stood, waiting.

The eight glass balls glowed, just a little bit. Dust motes floated through pale rays of light. The swirling water glimmered ever so slightly. The mirrors glimmered, too.

The air smelled of dust and dry old wood.

Something was supposed to happen. Bee just knew it.

But she felt nothing. Nothing moved.

Faintly, through the wood: "Mrow?"

With a deep sigh, she opened the door. What a bummer.

The cat was sitting on the desk now, tail curled round its paws as it yawned.

"It didn't work." She stared glumly at the cat. "Okay. One more time." Bee shut the door—more firmly now. She made sure the latch clicked.

Nothing.

"Never mind," she sighed. She lifted the latch—

And screamed as she fell into darkness.

*Chapter 15*
## ONE VERY SLOPPY PAGE

Federico paced the corridor as the bells of Santo Spirito rang midnight, his lantern sending anxious shapes across the closet door. In his other hand he gripped the key to the Sistine Chapel. He had so much to tell Herbert! How Herbert would laugh at Federico's tale of stealing the key—

*No,* Federico corrected himself with a smile. *Not stealing: obtaining.* To steal was wicked. He had simply borrowed the key for the sake of art. What better cause could there be? He'd return it, naturally. But only after he and Herbert—and Juno!—had climbed the scaffolding of the Sistine Chapel and admired Michelangelo's ceiling together.

*Bonngg,* went the bells. How many times had they rung? No matter; he'd see Herbert soon enough, with Juno in his arms. The thought of Juno made Federico smile doubly. Perhaps he could sneak her a treat from Master Bramante's plate—from under the architect's snoring nose. Obviously, the cat should not have run into the closet like that, particularly after he'd told her to stop. But now he knew better. Next time he'd make sure to keep her safe in his bedroom.

The last notes of Santo Spirito faded, so softly that the whole world seemed to end. Cautiously Federico opened the closet door. . . .

Empty.

Anxiety seeped from his belly to his throat. Where was Herbert?

*Bonngg,* went the bells of Santa Rufina. "At last," Federico whispered, wiping his forehead. Between each echoing toll, he listened. Was that a footstep?

Unable to wait a moment longer, he ripped open the door.

A boy fell out. A grimy young page. "Ow!" he howled, tumbling into the stack of tiles.

Federico checked the closet: still empty. "Where is 'Erbert?" he snapped, slipping the Sistine key into his cloak's secret pocket. One must hide everything of importance from pages.

The page sat rubbing his shin, muttering words Federico did not understand.

"Where is 'Erbert?" Federico repeated. "Where is Juno?"

"You know Italian? Wait—did you say Juno? And who's Erbert?" The page spoke with a coarse accent that Federico did not care for at all. Worse still was his uniform: old black hose and a shapeless jerkin with a crude crown symbol that Federico did not recognize, and he knew dozens of insignia. And the shoes! Two colors, to be certain, but made from cloth, with dirty edges and shapeless round toes, the laces uglier than ever he'd seen. Worst of all, the page had no cap.

"'Erbert. Meester Hh-er-bert Bot-ther," Federico spelled out.

"You mean Herbert Bother? Herbert Bother came here? Huh." The page turned to stare at the closet.

"Yes. Where is he?"

But now the page was gaping at the corridor with its

fine columns, at the marble floor and half-finished roof. "It worked," he whispered.

"I said, where is he?"

The page leaped to his feet. "I'm in Narnia!"

"What are you talking about?" Federico snapped. "You're in Rome, you fool. In the year of our Lord 1511." Herbert had appreciated that detail.

"I'm in Narnia!" The boy grabbed Federico. "Hey, are you Lucy?"

Federico snatched his arm away. "I am Sir Federico Gonzaga, heir to the throne of Mantua."

The page gawked at Federico's hose and shoulder-length hair. "Wait—you're not a girl?"

That did it. Federico had no choice but to slap him.

"Ow!" the page cried as if he'd never been struck—impossible, given his stupidity. "You hit me."

"I slapped you," Federico corrected. "And I'll slap you again if you do not behave. Here—"

The boy leaped back, smacking his elbow on the closet. "Ow. Dumb wardrobe."

Federico stiffened. "What did you call me?"

"I didn't call you anything. I called that"—he gestured to

the closet—"a wardrobe. You know, for fur coats? Haven't you ever read *The Lion, the Witch and the Wardrobe*?"

"*That* is a closet."

"No. A closet is built into a wall." The page drew a wall in the air. "But a wardrobe is like a box—" The page drew a box. "A big box that holds things. A box you can go through sometimes, to get to interesting places like Narnia where it's winter but then Lucy saves it and her brothers help—"

"Just tell me where 'Erbert is," Federico sighed.

The page's face fell.

Federico steeled himself. "I know. His hair is white this time. That wicked closet always makes him so old—"

"Herbert Bother is, um . . . dead."

Federico's heart stopped. "No, he's not."

"Yeah, he is. Like, fifty years ago? I'm sorry."

"That is impossible! He was here yesterday. He said he would see me this night—" Federico struggled to keep his voice from breaking. "And I saw Juno only moments ago—"

"You mean his cat?"

"She is my cat!" Federico did not want to sound so child-ish. "Not 'Erbert's. My cat. Mine!"

The page raised his hands. "Okay, okay. Whatever."

"She was here, just now." Federico jabbed at the closet. "Bring her back." He grabbed the page, pushing him forward. "It is special, this closet! It was made by Master Leonardo. So go get her—get them both—"

"Hey, let go of me!"

"Go to America Zhersey!" Dragging the page, he kicked open the door—

"Mrow."

Juno stood in the closet, her tail curled in a long cursive S. "Mrow," she greeted them both.

"Juno!" Federico shoved the page aside to grab her. "You're here! So 'Erbert must be alive, too." He rocked, burying his face in Juno's warm fur. "He has to be. He talks to me and brings me chocolate!" Juno gave his cheek a sympathetic lick. "He was *here*."

"I'm so sorry." The page looked about to cry. "That's really nice about the chocolate."

"And now I don't have anyone," Federico gulped. "I don't have anyone at all."

The page patted Federico's arm. "But you do. You have Miss Bother."

Abruptly Federico stopped rocking. "Who?"

"Miss Bother. Herbert's daughter. If Herbert means so much to you, then she's kind of like your sister."

"'Erbert does not have children," Federico declared in a voice of ice.

The page nodded helpfully. "Yes, he does. She was really sick and he adopted her—"

Federico dropped Juno, who stalked away in a huff. "He *adopted* her? That beggar girl?" He fell to his knees. "He adopted *her*?"

"But now she's really old and she's hurt and she's all by herself. It's really sad."

Federico pressed his face in his hands. "He adopted *her*?"

The page crouched beside him. Juno sat with her back to them both, angrily grooming her shoulder. "At least you don't have any broken bones. And you've got a nice place here—well, it'll be nice when it's done. All Miss Bother has is a falling-down house and Herbert's paintings, and a drawing she can't even sell—" He froze.

"What?" Federico snapped.

"Do you—" The page gulped. "This is Rome, right? Like, old Rome?"

"Yes, Rome." Federico swiped his tears. "And it's not old. It's 1511."

"Do you maybe know a painter named, um . . . Raphael?"

Federico snorted. "Of course I know Raphael! Why?"

The page looked at the corridor, the closet, at Federico's fine black cloak. "It's just that . . . I think Raphael is supposed to draw me."

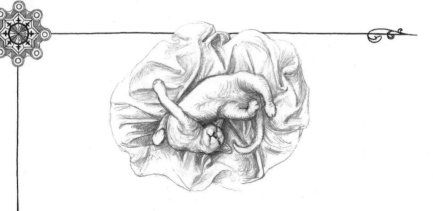

## *Chapter 16*
## A PLAN

Bee was trying her best to take it all in, crouched next to this snobby boy in a version of Rome that was five hundred years gone. The smells were so strong she could taste them: cook smoke and horse poop and spices and bread. Her ears caught the faint sounds of prayers, barking, church bells, banging. And the stars! Even with the glow of the moon, a million stars shone through the unfinished roof; moonlight turned ladders and planks into a ghostly parade. The glass balls in the wardrobe glowed, and the pale decorations on the door . . . wow.

Now Bee understood. The NO TIME PASSES note card,

and Miss Bother saying how her father went *back* to Rome . . . No wonder Herbert Bother had a Michelangelo drawing and a Raphael. All he had to do was stroll into the wardrobe and get them. *You'll make everything better,* Miss Bother had said to Bee as she was being wheeled into the ambulance. That wasn't a compliment. It was an order. The girl from the drawing had finally shown up. Now the girl from the drawing had to fix things. "It's just that . . . I think Raphael is supposed to draw me," she said.

Sir Federico climbed to his feet, swiping the tears from his face. "You?" He was the same size as Bee but he acted like he was a king.

"I think so."

Juno looked up at her. "Mrow."

Juno—Herbert's cat! Just like Miss Bother said. All those clues . . . "That's why I'm here, I think."

Federico lifted the lantern to study her face. "I've seen you before! In a drawing 'Erbert has—" His voice caught. "A drawing he *had.* He wanted Raphael to sign it—"

"But Raphael didn't." Bee's mind was spinning. "Not yet, anyway. That drawing? I'm pretty sure it's of me today." She touched the scratch on her neck. "Age eleven. Miss Bother has the drawing but she still needs his signature. So we need to find Raphael and get him to draw me—"

Federico frowned. "No, we don't. If your Botter person has the drawing, then Raphael already drew you."

"Yeah, but she has it in the future. It hasn't happened yet." Bee flapped her hands. "Just listen to me. This is what happens in time travel. He needs to draw me and sign it, then Miss Bother can sell it and her house won't be a wreck and she'll have the life she's supposed to." Bee could hug herself for figuring this out. "See?"

Federico pulled himself to his full height, adjusting his grip on the lantern. "It makes no difference to me."

"But everything fits together! The wardrobe, the drawing, 'age eleven,' Juno showing up the same time that I do . . . This is Herbert's daughter! She sleeps in her dining room and has envelopes that say URGENT. We have to help her—"

"*You* have to help her. *I* have to return to my room. I have a death to mourn. Come, girl." He snapped his fingers at Juno lounging in a moonbeam.

Bee couldn't believe it. What would persuade him? "That drawing is worth a lot of money, you know."

Federico flipped back his cloak. "I have more than enough wealth."

"What about chocolate?"

Federico paused. "And peanuts?" He turned away, setting his jaw. "No."

"What, then?" Bee stomped around to face him. "What can I do to get you to help me?"

"You can get me my friend!" he snarled. "Juno? Now!"

With a yawn and a stretch, Juno rose to her feet, rubbing the edge of the wardrobe.

Frantically Federico waved at her. "Juno! Get away from that evil contraption!"

*Huh,* Bee thought. *Fancy-pants is scared of the wardrobe.* Grandpa Pepe said to find your enemy's weakness. "Fine," she declared, marching to the wardrobe door.

"Fine," Federico mimicked. "And good riddance. You've no need to ever return."

"Oh, I'm not leaving." Bee wiggled the door latch. "Here, kitty." She snapped her fingers.

Juno's ears pricked up. "Mrow?" She sauntered over.

Federico froze. "What are you doing?"

"I can't get Herbert, but we can save his daughter." Bee eased the wardrobe door open. "I told you: that's why I'm here."

"Mrow?" Juno sniffed at the air.

"No!" Federico shrieked. "Don't do that—"

A shadow of movement—and like that, Juno was gone.

"You monster!" Federico shouted, reaching for his knife.

Bee leaped back just in time, scrambling onto a stack of lumber, and from there to the top of the wardrobe. "I'll bring Juno back I promise I swear it!" she cried. Wow, did he look mad. And he had a knife!

"How?" he spat. "She'll die, too—"

"No, she won't. No time passes. She'll be fine. All we need is to get Raphael to draw me and make sure he signs it. It's that simple."

Federico glowered up at her. "I don't need you, you know. I could simply go get her myself."

Bee gestured grandly to the door at her feet. "Go for it. Be my guest."

Federico scowled at the wardrobe. He didn't move. "I have no concern for that beggar girl."

"Miss Bother isn't a girl anymore—" But it didn't matter how old Miss Bother was. She still needed help. "Herbert would want this. You know he would."

"'Erbert," Federico whispered. Slowly he returned the knife to his belt. "'Erbert . . ."

Bee crept to the front edge of the wardrobe. "He couldn't come back, you know."

Federico's head came up. "What?"

"Miss Bother told me. She said Herbert always wanted to come back here but he couldn't, and that it made him really sad."

Federico brightened. "He wanted to see me again?"

"Well, yeah. Who wouldn't?" Cautiously she climbed down.

Federico stared at the wardrobe as if willing Herbert to walk through it. "He loved that drawing. It was like a quest for him, getting the signature."

"Yeah." Bee liked that: a quest.

Federico smoothed his doublet. "I helped save the beggar child, you know. I held this door. I prayed. I, too, care for the drawing."

"That's good." Was he agreeing?

Federico sighed. "As my mother always says, it is cunning and diplomacy that preserve the smaller states." He held out the lantern.

"Wait—what?" And then, more politely, "Excuse me?"

"Carry this." He shook the lantern impatiently.

Confused, Bee took it. "Wow, this is heavy—"

Federico flipped his cloak over his shoulder. "It shall be your task henceforth to bear my possessions." He set off down the corridor, not looking back. "We shall suffer as allies till Juno is mine."

# PART III

# PLANS FAIL

## Chapter 17
## FRED

Federico strode down the dark corridor toward the villa. The page lumbered behind, swinging the lantern as if he'd never carried a light. Now that Federico was in charge, he felt much better. It was a dreadful situation, to be sure; the news about Herbert had broken his heart. But he must not dwell. However he felt about that beggar girl, he needed his cat. He must focus like a warrior on the battle at hand. "We shall spend tonight in my villa," he declared. He'd secure the page in the storeroom. "Tomorrow we meet Raphael." God willing, he'd have Juno home by dusk.

"Tomorrow? That's so far away—" The page relaxed.

"Wait. No time passes." He peered out a window. "I have time to look around."

"That is His Holiness's private garden," Federico explained. "He has a magnificent collection of sculptures." The moonlight caught the marble quite prettily.

"There are so many stars!"

Federico sighed. "In order to see statues, one needs to look down."

The page trotted across the corridor to lean out the window on the opposite side. "That's Rome, right? It's so dark."

"Yes. Because it is nighttime." Would Federico have to explain everything? The moon illuminated the towers and rooftops, the distant mountains, the slow-moving river. The streets, however, would be dark enough. He shivered at the memory of his perilous trip with Herbert.

"There aren't any lights. That's crazy."

"It is sane," Federico corrected. "Candles are dangerous and very expensive." He nodded at the crude crown on the boy's jerkin. "Does your master waste candles at midnight?"

"My master?" The page peered down at the insignia. "Oh, the crown is because of my nickname. Queen Bee—because of Beatrice? The joke works better in English."

That made sense. The page was quite like a bee: annoying. But—

"Your name is Beatrice?" He stared at the page. "You're a girl? But the drawing . . ."

The page scowled. "What's wrong with girls?"

"Well, nothing," Federico lied. "But girls don't look like you. They stay out of the sun, and wear their hair long, and practice sewing."

"Not me."

Heavens, but he—she—had a fierce glare.

"They have chaperones, and do not wear hose."

"They're called leggings."

He pointed at the girl's feet. "They wear slippers, not . . ."

"High-tops. It's a kind of sneaker. For basketball and running around."

"Girls do not 'run around.'" Federico studied the jerkin and dirty black *leggings*. "You're not even a page, are you?"

Beatrice scowled at him. "What's a page?"

"Ah." That explained the incompetence. "A page is a servant, a personal attendant who's well trained. . . . Anyway, let us continue." Federico walked, pondering this revelation, as the girl gaped at every ladder and nail. "How much is your dowry?" A girl so filthy and uneducated wouldn't have much, but he should be polite.

The girl poked at a tub of sand. "What are you talking about?"

"A dowry is the money a woman brings to her marriage. My mother brought three thousand ducats and three chests of silver and—"

"We don't do that anymore." She brushed off her hands, sending the lantern swinging. "That's, like, medieval."

"It is supremely important! How else will people know your family's worth? How will you live when your husband dies?"

The girl barked a laugh. "Um, I'm not married? So it doesn't matter?"

How brave she acted. Every woman needed a dowry. Even peasants. To pretend it didn't matter . . . "Ah, Beatrice," he sighed.

"Just say Bee. No one calls me Beatrice except Miss Bother. And I'll call you . . . Fred."

"My father," Federico said coldly, "is Francesco the Second, the foremost knight in Italy, ruler of Mantua and head of the family Gonzaga. My mother is the daughter of the Duke of Ferrara and a renowned collector of art. Her sister was the

Duchess of Milan. My father's brother is a cardinal, and my aunts have all married dukes."

"Where does that go?" Bee held the lantern up to a small door in a niche.

"You are missing my point," Federico snapped. "I am not 'Fred,' I am—"

"Is that, like, a secret portal?" Bee interrupted.

Federico snorted. "Hardly. It leads to the studio of a sculptor named Michelangelo."

"Michelangelo?" Bee stared at him, wide-eyed.

"Ah." Federico had impressed her at last. "In fact, I know him well."

"Wow," she breathed. "I know someone who knows Michelangelo."

This girl was like Herbert, then: awed by art. "You don't happen to know an artist named Leonardo da Vinci, do you?" he asked, as casually as he could. "The genius who designed the closet?"

"Of course I know da Vinci—wait, he designed the wardrobe?" Her eyes got even wider. "That makes so much sense."

"Yes, well, he lived in my family's castle."

"No way, really? What's he like?" She blinked. "Wait—your family has a castle?"

"Of course." Federico flicked a bit of dust from his cuff. "To be honest, Master Leonardo lived there before I was born. But my mother still speaks of a pink cloak that he wore."

Bee shook her head. "That's amazing. You must be so famous."

Federico smoothed his doublet. How fine it felt to be well regarded.

On they walked. Bee held the lantern with a bit more skill so that the shadows no longer lurched. She inhaled, smiling, and Federico could smell it, too: orange blossoms. They were nearly at the villa. "You'll have to come with me to my room," he conceded. He could not lock this girl in a storeroom.

"Okay. But won't your mother be mad?"

"My mother lives hundreds of miles away. I am a hostage of His Holiness while my father commands the pope's army."

"You're a *hostage*?" Bee raised the lantern, almost smacking him. "You must be really brave."

Well. He'd been wise indeed to keep her out of the storeroom. "Shh. We are here." Taking the lantern, he eased open the villa door. Silently he led her to his bedroom, listening for

Celeste's sleeping wheeze. "This is the bedroom His Holiness gave me," he whispered, turning the lantern so Bee could see his father's portrait, the antiques he'd collected, his finely carved travel chest.

"Wow." Bee brushed her fingertips across a tapestry with a golden-threaded unicorn. "I love this."

"Me, too." He talked to the unicorn sometimes, though he'd never admit it.

Bee stroked the tassels on the bed. "It's so soft."

Federico opened his travel chest. "Of course. I picked out the fabric myself." Checking that the Sistine Chapel key was secure in the secret pocket, he packed the cloak away.

"Um, excuse me. Where should I sleep?"

"The bed, naturally. I would not make a girl use the floor." Blowing out the lantern, he climbed under the covers. "We must be sure to wake before Celeste. She's my governess." How fine it felt to whisper in the dark. How he'd missed it. "When I was a child in Mantua, I would sleep with my little sisters. Three peas in a pod, Celeste called us. Livia always held my hand till she fell asleep."

Bee burrowed under the covers. "Do you miss her?"

"I always miss her." It took him a moment to speak.

"Three years ago she passed to God."

Bee swallowed. "That's awful. I'm sorry."

*Herbert passed as well,* he thought. But it hurt too much to say this out loud. "Your Italian is quite good," he said instead. "Although different."

"I spend every summer in Italy. My grandparents have a farm my great-grandfather bought."

He snuggled deeper between the sheets. "My great-grand-father was the King of Naples."

Bee snorted. "That's funny."

"But it's on my mother's side." Federico yawned. "So I don't have a claim."

Bee sat up. "Wait—you're serious?"

"Stop it." He tugged at the bedspread. "You are mussing the cover."

"That's amazing." She settled back down. "Hey, you know what? This is fun."

Federico smiled into the darkness.

Bee wriggled into her pillow. "Goodnight, Fred."

Federico yawned to split his face. "Goodnight, Bee." He wished he had Juno curled up beside him. But till his cat came back, this strange girl would do.

## Chapter 18
## BEDSIDE VIEW

Bee lay in the broad soft bed, absolutely twitching. How could Fred just go to sleep? This was the most exciting thing in the whole wide world. She, Beatrice Rosetti Bliss, was a time traveler—using a machine made by da Vinci himself! Wow. Wow. Wow.

No wonder Miss Bother had freaked when she saw Bee. No wonder she freaked about the cat. All her life, Miss Bother had been waiting for Juno and Bee. And then out of the blue, they showed up! *You'll make everything better*, Miss Bother had said. Well, Bee absolutely would. One hundred percent. Raphael, drawing, done. Then she'd go back to her own time in New Jersey because NO TIME PASSES and Miss Bother would have the drawing and Fred would have Juno and Bee wouldn't even have to explain to Mom and Moo!

She'd tell Nonna, though, when Nonna and Pepe got back from their cruise. Grandma Nonna loved stories. And she could keep a secret. She never even told Moo about that time Bee drove the car.

Fred made a snuffling sound. For a bossy kid, he was okay. It was really sad about his sister. Bee peered through the darkness, trying to see the guy in black armor. What a creepy painting. How could anyone sleep with that in their bedroom? Or with all that snoring in the next room? Or with the whole city of Rome right outside? She wasn't going to sleep a wink—

She woke up to a kick in her ribs. "Get out!" a voice demanded.

"Wha. . . ?" Bee mumbled. Bright daylight shone in her eyes.

"Under the bed!" Another kick, and Bee tumbled to the floor. Luckily she fell onto carpet. "Quick," the voice commanded, and without thinking Bee rolled under the bed. Not a moment too soon, for in scurried a woman who talked without taking a breath.

"Still asleep, my lord? Look at you abed with the day half done, and such a tangle of sheets. I'd like a word with His Holiness about the hours he keeps, for they do not suit a growing boy. Shall you wear your watered silk? Though I am not sure about dove gray for the hose. Perhaps saffron would be more suitable. . . ." On and on she went, her slippers shuffling back and forth.

"Yes, Celeste. No, Celeste," a boy answered. Fred! Sir Federico Gonzaga. Bee shivered in glee. And she was lying under Fred's bed, five hundred years ago in the middle of Rome!

The woman paused. "Did you hear a noise, my lord?" She stooped to peer under the bed.

Bee scrambled backward. Where to hide? There was nothing but dust.

"No, Celeste!" Fred yammered. "It's the cat—the wind— my father's portrait! Look: behold him. Is he not fearsome?"

A woman's scarfed head came into view, blocked by Fred's legs. "I cannot see—"

"Nothing is there, I vow it. Is not Papa's portrait fine?"

The woman straightened with a grunt. "The portrait has always been fine," she grumbled.

*Dummy,* Bee scolded herself. *Don't make noise.* She just

needed to relax and be quiet and wait until they could meet Raphael. And pay attention to everything, duh, because she was a time traveler! Even if she was stuck under a bed. Fred's bedroom looked really nice, actually, at least what she could see of it. The portrait hung over a desk next to a gui-tar-thing—a lute. A white marble statue looked like something in a museum. She should take a picture for Moo—

But wait—there weren't any cameras in the 1500s. Or phones.

Fred peered under the bed, his blond hair tousled. "How are you?" he whispered.

She gave him a thumbs-up. "Great!"

"My lord, what are you doing?"

Fred jumped to his feet. "I'm checking on Juno."

"That yellowed-eyed demon? 'Tis a wonder we have not died in our sleep thanks to her; she gives me nightmares, I'm sure. Now come—"

"I hope the cat's doing well." Fred stamped his foot. "I am anxious to see her."

Bee frowned at his foot. Of course she remembered their deal! Once the drawing was done, Fred could have Juno forever.

"Hold still so I may fasten your belt. Saints above but you are a-wiggle today. And behold, here is the master. You shall sit still for him, I trust."

Bee watched from under the bed as Fred sat at the desk, reading aloud. A sniffling old man stood over him, bopping Fred with a stick whenever he made a mistake. Celeste sat next to them, sewing.

What kind of place was this?

Bee craned her head, trying to see.

"You are not paying attention." Celeste rapped Fred on the head with her thimble. "You must attend."

Fred nodded, not even flinching. Not upset that he kept getting hit. Poor kid.

"I have a letter from your mother, my lord," the sniffly old man announced.

Fred's head came up. "A letter? Why did you not tell me?"

"'Tis only a portion. The greater part was written to me." He cleared his throat noisily.

> *Dearest son, We are delighted to read of your progress in Latin, and hope your tutors do not need to use their sticks. We know you represent well the house of Gonzaga.*

*Your father, the duke, knows this also. We send three new*
*undershirts and a belt that is a gift from our brother.*

The old man tucked the letter into his vest. "That is all."

"Isn't that nice?" Celeste declared, not looking up.

"I should like to read it myself—" Fred began.

"Did you not hear?" The tutor rapped Fred's head. "You must continue. Second paragraph, please. Erant omnino itinera duo. . . ."

Fred sighed, shoulders drooping. *"There were two streets—"*

"Routes, my lord." Bop.

Bee clenched her fists. Why didn't Fred get mad?

She tried to get comfortable on the floor. She could hear music in the distance, and birds, but mostly she heard construction. Hammering and clanging and men shouting, "One, two, three, pull." She wished she could see what they were pulling. It had to be more interesting than Latin. Also she really needed to pee.

No one in books ever talked about pee.

Fred plodded through his lesson. Even the old man wasn't listening, but whispering to Celeste about someone's girlfriend—or boyfriend? Bee couldn't make out the words. Fred tried to sneak a glance under the bed, and Celeste smacked him. "Stop looking for that beast, my lord. 'Tis shocking," she murmured to the tutor. "I would never repeat such a tale."

Fred snuck another glance. Bee made a face as she pointed to her, you know, bladder area. What was the gesture for *I really need to pee?*

Fred looked away, frowning. He tapped his pen against the table.

"Stop it, my lord." The old man rapped him. "You will damage the nib."

"Yes! That is it. I need fresh nibs. Get them, now, please. I demand it."

"But my lord, 'tis quite a distance—"

"How can a gentleman have perfect penmanship without perfect pens? My mother says this often." He almost pushed the man out of the room. "And Celeste? I should like the ginger syrup she sent me. I have quite a yearning."

Celeste continued stitching. "The ginger is for when you are sick."

Fred drew himself up. "Perhaps I am sick. Perhaps it is one of those illnesses that appears without warning and renders me dead. Heaven forbid."

Quickly Celeste reached for his forehead. "Oh, my lord, do not speak so!"

He pulled away. "We cannot be too safe. The ginger, please. I insist." He crossed his arms.

Bee watched, stunned. If she talked like that to Moo, she'd be in so much trouble. Or Mom? Yikes. But things were different here, obviously. The servants bossed Fred around and hit him. But he bossed them, too. It was so complicated.

Celeste frowned. "'Tis on a high shelf in the storage room. I shall need a stool to reach it."

Fred raised an eyebrow. "We have always thought you capable of such feats. But perhaps we are mistaken."

"I am quite capable, my lord, thank you." Celeste marched from the room, her mouth a line.

As soon as she was out of sight, Fred dropped to his knees. "Quick, Bee!" He pointed to a carved wooden screen in the corner. "There. Hurry."

Bee didn't need to be told twice. She wiggled out and Fred dragged her to her feet and pushed her behind the screen—

"Found it." Celeste bustled back in. "The jar was lower than I feared."

Bee froze. What should she do now? There was nothing

behind the screen but a pot with a lid. She needed a bath-room, not a pot.

Oh.

"How clever you are. Thank you, Celeste. Set it on my desk, if you please."

Bee glared at the pot. This was so gross. But not as gross as wetting her pants. Holding her nose, she lifted the lid. Empty, whew.

"I say, Celeste, shall we sing together? The Lord's Prayer. It's my mother's favorite." Loudly Fred began.

With a sigh, Bee pulled down her leggings. She didn't have much time—Fred couldn't sing forever. She sat on the chamber pot, wincing at the cold. No one ever talked about *this* in books.

"Why aren't you singing, Celeste? My mother will be so pleased. And look, here is my Latin master, returned already. Heavens, that was fast."

As quietly as she could, Bee began to pee.

## Chapter 19
# THE NEW SERVANT

It was all Federico could do to keep his eyes from the screen. He'd been quite brilliant in solving Bee's predicament. But she could not stay there forever. What if Celeste or Master Sniffly looked behind it? What if Bee made a noise?

"You are not paying attention," Master Sniffly scolded, rapping Federico.

Federico pushed himself away from the desk. He could not thread two thoughts together with all this distraction! *If you act like a lord,* his mother said, *then so you will be treated.* "I should like my lunch now. A large lunch, if you please."

To his absolute shock, they agreed. Celeste and Master

Sniffy never listened! But perhaps, Federico mused, he had never before been so forceful.

"I shall visit Raphael this afternoon," he added as footmen carried in trays. The wooden screen, he noticed, trembled ever so slightly at this news.

"But you have a lute lesson, and fencing." Master Sniffly sniffed. "You mustn't waste your time on unimportant matters."

Federico drew himself up. "Shall I tell my mother, the most celebrated collector in Italy, that you consider art unimportant?" He felt rather like a swordsman turning a parry into a jab as he used Master Sniffly's words against him, and sure enough the Latin master rushed to take back his statement. Feigning insult, Federico herded Master Sniffly and Celeste from the room. He slumped against the door, feeling as though he'd just completed a full day of jousting. How exhausting it was to be sly.

"Are they gone?" a voice whispered from behind the screen as the last footman departed.

"Yes!" Federico announced. "Please join me." How fine the table looked with china and gleaming silver. Sometimes a day of jousting ended quite well. He inhaled, taking in the scents of saffron, pepper, nutmeg, sage. . . .

"Wow." Bee's eyes widened at the spread of platters. Her

eyes stopped at a finely roasted bird. "Um, what's that?"

Federico beamed. "Partridge stuffed with apricots. Have you never seen this delicacy? It's one of my favorites." He sliced the meat, arranging it just so. How gifted he was at carving.

"A partridge?" Bee gulped. "Like in a pear tree?"

"I suppose. They are ground-nesters but on occasion they sit in trees."

"And that?" Her frown grew.

"Peacock in gold sauce. Though the sauce in this case is made from saffron and egg yolks. Gold is only for banquets. And starlings in jelly—"

"Peacocks? Starlings?" Bee stepped back.

"Why, yes. And here are doves in parsley sauce—"

"Doves?" Bee looked crushed. "I don't eat doves."

"Ah." Bravely Federico continued. "I also have ravioli with pumpkin, and melons with ham, and pudding baked with sugar for they know I like sweetness. And look." He held up a piece of silverware. "This is called a *fork*. I can show you how to operate it."

"Um, I think I'm okay with forks." Bee eased into a chair. "Can I please just have some melon?"

"But you must eat it with ham or it will rot in your stomach."

Bee paused. "It will rot in my stomach?"

"Everyone knows this. Surely I can tempt you with another dish—perhaps macaroni in the style of Naples?"

Bee twirled a forkful of the macaroni. She was pretty good with a fork, he had to admit. "We call it spaghetti where I come from. But usually it has tomato sauce—" She gagged. "Ugh, cinnamon sugar."

"But sugar and cinnamon are both expensive and delicious." Federico was so confused! "So what do you eat in your country that is special?"

"I'm sorry." To her credit, Bee looked very contrite. "We love cinnamon where I come from. And sugar. And lots of people eat birds. Just not doves. Or"—she gulped—"peacocks." She speared a ravioli. "But I love these."

"I do as well." In truth pumpkin made Federico retch, but he did not want to sound rude.

She tore off a piece of bread. "Wow, this bread rocks—I mean, it's delicious. It's great." She smiled at him through a mouthful. "So how long till we go see Raphael?"

"We?" Federico frowned, slicing the ham. "But you cannot walk through His Holiness's palace."

"Why not? Because I'm a girl?" The prickliness had returned to her voice.

"Certainly not." No one would think her a girl in that outfit—she looked more like a rag-picker with her bare head and cloth shoes. "Because the entire palace would gossip."

"But how can Raphael draw me if he can't even see me?"

"Ah." Federico had been so focused on Juno. . . . "I know. I shall ask him to visit me here."

"Wow. He'd do that for you?"

Federico squirmed. "I should like to think so." Truly he should have given more thought to a plan.

"Today?" Bee asked. "Because he has to draw me now."

"Shh. Do you want servants in the villa to hear? That's it!" Federico leaped from his chair to dig through his travel chest. "You'll be a servant." He himself had mistaken her for a page last night. Others would, too.

"A servant? Awesome!" She knelt to help him.

"Stop it. You're mussing the folds." He handed her a bundle.

"They're so cool!" She started to take off her black saggy top. "You can't watch me change, though."

"But—as you wish." Federico turned around, waiting impatiently. He could not resist a peak. Bee looked quite smart in a linen shirt with a sleeveless gray jerkin. "What is that?" He leaned over to see.

"It's underwear." She stepped back. "What are you doing?"

Federico bent closer. "Is it embroidered?"

"It doesn't matter. They're just little flowers, okay?"

*"It doesn't matter?"* Federico stared at her, incredulous. "It always matters."

"Stop it!" She turned away, tugging at the hose. "These don't stay up."

"Have you never dressed yourself? You forgot your strap." He tied a strap round her waist. "You attach them thus." He looped each hose to the strap and pulled down the jerkin. "Done."

"Thank you. Hey, look at that." She lifted a foot to marvel at the leather sole sewn to the end of her hose. "The socks have shoes built right in."

The things this girl didn't know. Naturally hose had built-in shoes; that was how well-born folk dressed. Federico fastened a midnight-blue belt and knife over her jerkin. "Grand. And when you bow . . ."

Bee bowed.

Federico winced. "Don't bow. Or if you must, do it exactly like that. People will take pity. Say you were sent by the Duchess of Urbino."

"Who's she?"

He adjusted her collar. "A relative with no brains at all."

"Thanks." Her face softened. "I mean it. Thank you."

"The pleasure is mine." He set a gray cap on her head. "There. Now you are fit to meet Raphael. You'll like him very much."

She bent over, peering at her legs. "Can you see my underwear?"

"No one cares about a servant's underwear—" He caught sight of her face. "I mean, no." He picked up a small silver tray. "Carry this." He held it up on two hands, to demonstrate.

"Wait—what? Why?"

"Because you are my servant, naturally." He donned his blue cap edged with pearls. "Thus you walk behind me, carrying an item of value." He checked himself in the mirror, tying on his sky-blue cloak with cream silk lining and ermine trim. Was he perfect? Yes.

Bee held up the tray as if it were made out of glass, or poison. Federico sighed to himself. Tossing back his cloak, he opened the door to let them both out.

## Chapter 20

# HEAVILY GUARDED

Bee hurried through the villa after Fred, doing her best not to slip. The marble floors were so smooth, and her hose-shoes didn't have the best grip. Painted cupids romped on the ceiling above them, fluttering between white fluffy clouds. The smell of orange blossoms drifted through the open windows. A hedge of glossy-leafed orange trees held fruits that glowed like tiny suns.

Fred passed two women scrubbing the floor, Bee scampering behind with the tray. "My lord," they cried, jumping up to curtsey. They wore layers of skirts but no shoes. Fred walked right by, not even acknowledging them. Should Bee say hello? She wasn't sure.

They passed a man carrying a stack of books. "My lord." The man bowed. Again Fred didn't seem to notice. His face was weird. Like he was wearing a mask, Bee realized. Like he was so heavily guarded, just within himself, that he couldn't even respond. "My lord," the man repeated. "A moment, please?"

Fred kept walking. Bee scurried after him, head down.

"My lord! My lord—"

Chin up, Fred marched around the corner, Bee at his heels.

"My lord . . ." The man's voice faded.

"Wow." Bee's heart was beating like she'd just finished a sprint.

"Shh," Fred murmured, face smooth. He heaved open a door. The corridor! Bee recognized it from last night.

Fred shut the door behind them, and immediately his shoulders relaxed; his mask melted away. "You should see yourself," he chuckled, imitating her face scrunched in fear.

"What? I've never done this before."

"Don't worry, you're fine. Anyway, no one will see us here." He walked beside her, pointing out a window. "His Holiness's garden. You may see it clearly now in the daylight."

"Wow. Moo would love this." White statues stood between

skinny trees, dark green against the rich blue sky. Workmen dug out a hillside. In the distance rose a jumble of windows and arches and towers. The palace.

"Let us continue walking. Who is this Moo, if you please? Your cow?"

Bee laughed. "One of my moms."

"You have two mothers?"

"We're like any family. We have breakfast together and Moo makes my lunch and Mom walks me to school. . . ."

Fred just stood there. She could almost see his brain whirling, he was thinking so hard. "Which one has the dowry?"

A long moment of silence. "What?" Bee asked, finally.

"The dowry, the dowry!" He gestured helplessly. "Why do you pretend it does not matter? Which of your mothers brought wealth to their marriage?"

For a second—just one second—Bee wanted to bop him on the head with the tray. "How many times do I have to tell you? We. Don't. Have. Dowries."

"Keep your voice down—"

"I. Am."

They continued onward. Fred looked like he might never speak again.

They passed the little door set in the niche. "Does that really go to Michelangelo's studio?" Bee asked, to break the silence.

Fred brightened. "But of course. His Holiness likes to visit. He tells Michelangelo what to do and Michelangelo ignores him. One time Michelangelo got so angry that he threw a plank at his head."

"Wow. Now I really want to call Moo." Bee sighed. "What's it like not having your mom around? Because I talk to mine all the time. Like, *all* the time."

Fred's face went smooth. "We communicate. You heard her letter this morning."

"Yeah, but it wasn't an 'I love you I miss you' kind of letter. . . . Although my moms can be bossy, too," she hurried to add. "There was this one time we were in the Sistine Chapel—"

Fred's head snapped around. "You know the Sistine Chapel?"

"Sure. And there was this group of Japanese tourists—"

"What is Japanese?"

"People from Japan? Maybe you don't know Japan yet. It's near China. It was so embarrassing. Moo started telling them about Adam—you know, the scene of Adam and Eve in the garden?"

Fred smiled proudly. "I watched Master Michelangelo put the final touches on that scene."

"Wow." Bee paused for a moment. "That's amazing. Anyway, Moo made me pose." She spread her arms to demonstrate. "She gave a whole lecture on how excited he was to eat the apple."

Fred sighed. "Two mothers must mean twice as many lectures."

"It wasn't that kind of lecture, but I know what you're talking about. Last week I climbed a tree and she got so mad."

"But of course. Girls don't climb trees."

"That's not what I mean—"

Fred frowned, staring up the corridor. There, not too far ahead, was the wardrobe. But someone was crawling behind it!

Fred dashed forward, hand on his knife. "I beg your pardon!"

Hastily a man stood up—an older man with white hair and a thick belly.

At once Fred took his hand off his knife, his face cool. "Good afternoon, Master Bramante."

Bramante . . . Bee knew that name, didn't she? Maybe Moo studied him. Moo studied so many people. Bee couldn't keep track of them all.

"Forgive me, my lord." Smugly the white-haired man waved a paper. "I have just received a letter from my dear friend, Leonardo da Vinci—"

Bee gasped. Did everyone here know da Vinci?

Bramante scowled at her interruption. "How rude your servant is."

Bee ducked, blushing, but Fred only shrugged. "He came from the Duchess of Urbino."

"Ah. I see." Bramante returned his gaze to the wardrobe. "Master Leonardo has asked me to examine it." He lowered his voice. "He is looking for . . . a cat."

Wait—what? Bee shot Fred a look.

Fred smiled evenly. "Master Leonardo asked you to find a cat in a closet? How peculiar."

Bramante frowned at the letter, absently jangling his heavy ring of keys. "A kitten, really. He thinks a kitten is stuck in there somehow."

"Very peculiar indeed." Fred kept looking at the keys, Bee noticed. "Have you ever heard of such a thing?" he asked her. Quickly Bee shook her head.

Suddenly a door slammed behind them—so loudly that she jumped, and Fred, and Bramante. "What is this toad of an architect doing?" a man snarled.

Fred regained his composure first. "Ah, Master Michelangelo. How fare you today?"

Bee stared at the man stomping up the corridor with a fistful of hammers. This was Michelangelo? "I forgot these," he barked. His nose lay flat against his face, and paint spattered his clothes. He'd spent so much time looking up at the Sistine Chapel ceiling that he couldn't even straighten his neck. There was something weird about him, she remembered, like he never washed his hands. . . .

The smell hit her. "Ugh," she wheezed, grabbing her nose.

His head tipped back, Michelangelo sneered over his chin at Bramante. "I said, what are you doing here?"

Bramante stiffened. "I have every right to be here. I designed this corridor."

"Of course you did," Michelangelo spat. "Which is why it's so . . . so bad."

Oh, yeah: that was another thing about Michelangelo. He was kind of a grouch.

Bramante flicked his cloak. "That's your best insult, Master Michelangelo? That it's 'bad'? You don't have the wit to work in Rome."

Michelangelo tightened his grip on the hammers. Ropes of muscles ran up his arms. His shoulders, Bee noticed, strained against his shirt.

"Although you are a great talent," Bramante stumbled to add. "We all say it."

"I'm a genius," Michelangelo corrected. But he lowered the hammers. "At least I finish my work, unlike Leonardo da Vinci." He nodded at Fred. "Good day, Federico. Beware this toad and his peacock." Away he stomped, his cloud of stink almost visible.

Bramante stuck out his tongue at Michelangelo's back. He marched off in the other direction, jangling his keys.

"Wow," Bee whispered. "Those guys really hate each other."

Fred couldn't help grinning. "How observant you are. . . . Shall we continue?"

"What was that about a kitten?" Bee held up the tray, trying to look servant-like. They were almost at the end of the corridor. "Bramante wasn't talking about Juno, was he?"

Fred nodded. "She is—she was—Master Leonardo's cat. Before she was mine."

"Da Vinci's cat? Wow. She really is special."

"She is." Fred beamed with pride. They had reached the door. "Let us find this peacock and convince him to draw you."

"Absolutely," Bee agreed. "But, um, who's the peacock again?"

Fred heaved the door open. "Raphael, of course. It's Michelangelo's nickname for him."

"Wait—what?" Bee lowered the tray in surprise.

Fred winced. "We are entering His Holiness's palace. Please try not to look . . . incompetent."

"I know, I know." Bee hurried back into her pose. "It's just that Herbert hid Raphael's drawing behind a painting of a peacock." She shook her head, following Fred through the door. "It's like an enormous jigsaw puzzle," she said, more to herself. If only they'd be able to find all the pieces.

## Chapter 21
# THE DEAL

Federico led Bee into the great clanging ruckus of construc‑
tion. Plasterers lugged tubs past a bellowing foreman; a pigment
grinder sang a bawdy tune as he pounded rocks into colorful
powder; pairs of men stomped through the workrooms bearing
timbers on their broad padded shoulders.

As soon as they caught sight of Federico, the men hurried to
doff their caps. Federico barely nodded, though inside he beamed
at the recognition. "Take me to Master Raphael, if you please," he
asked the foreman, stepping between tubs of thick, stinky plaster.

"I've been here," Bee whispered, gaping at the painting of
Swiss Guards.

"Ah," said Federico. So had Herbert. "Now please hush."

Bee pressed her lips together, but she gawked as they entered the next room. "I know this, too," she said without moving her mouth.

"It's His Holiness's study," Federico muttered back. "That wall is *The School of Athens*." He watched her eyes, but she did not seem to notice his likeness. He'd point it out later.

The room swarmed with painters laboring on every blank surface; one brave soul dabbed at the ceiling from the top of a ladder. Raphael stood holding a paintbrush, gesturing to a woman with her arms gracefully posed. "Do you see?" he asked the other painters. "Do you see the curl of her exquisite lips?"

The model laughed, her eyes sparkling.

"Do not laugh, my lovely. It makes you too beautiful." Raphael dipped his brush in a pot of paint, and with three quick strokes he captured the shape of her mouth. "There."

Federico inhaled with delight. He could not tell which was more perfect: the woman or the image painted on the wall. And Raphael captured her smile with only three strokes! Such talent.

"Sir Federico, what a joy." Wiping his hands, Raphael

strolled over. "I cannot recall you ever looking better." He tucked a curl beneath Bee's cap. "There. Now your servant is flawless."

Bee blushed, ducking to hide her smile.

The artist made a show of peering about. "And where, pray tell, is your lioness?"

"My lioness? Ah, my cat. Juno. She is . . . waiting for me." Federico gave Bee a pointed look. "I hope to see her very soon. In fact, Master, I have come to ask a favor."

Raphael leaned back, arms crossed. "Say the word, my lord. Your wish is my command."

"Yes. Ah." Federico gestured to Bee. "Here, as you see, is my new page, from the Duchess of Urbino. The duchess is very fond of h·him."

"I can see why. Such a handsome face." Raphael smiled at Bee's embarrassment.

"Yes. So." Federico gulped. "We would like you to draw him."

Raphael raised an eyebrow. "To draw him?"

"Yes, please." Bee bobbed her ghastly bow. "In ink, please. With your signature."

Federico nudged Bee: *quiet!* "We would need it quite soon."

Raphael laughed. "I'd love to. But as you can see, I have

ten painters to manage. I have a dozen patrons beyond His Holiness, including your mother. I have her." He nodded to the woman who smiled back, twirling a strand of hair. "What can you offer?"

"How much money do you have?" Bee whispered.

"Not enough." Raphael chuckled, overhearing. "Time, as you know, is never free."

Ah. This was why Raphael could afford ten assistants and the prettiest model in Rome. The artist was talented and kind and graceful . . . but he was also an excellent business-man. "I . . . know people." Federico stammered. He could not think of what else to offer.

"You do." Raphael paused, considering him. "You know the dark one."

Federico shared a confused look with Bee. "Satan?"

Raphael clapped his hands. "Ha, that is brilliant. I'm afraid I refer to the other devil. Michelangelo. He likes you, and he doesn't like anyone. Me, he hates especially. Show me his precious ceiling and you'll have your drawing."

"But Master Michelangelo forbids it." Federico shuddered, remembering Michelangelo's wrath. "Besides, the chapel is locked. It's imposs—"

He slapped a palm over his mouth. No, it wasn't impossible. He had a key to the Sistine Chapel in a secret pocket at the bottom of his travel chest. "Done," he said, holding out his hand.

Raphael's eyebrows went up. "I had not realized my lord was such a man of action."

Bee squirmed beside Federico. "We, um, need it *now*—"

Gently Federico stepped on her foot. "When might you manage this?" he asked Raphael. "It would be nice to have it soon."

Raphael stroked his chin. "Hmm. Tonight, let us say. After sunset, when the dark one has left for the day."

"Tonight?" Bee looked crushed. "That's hours away."

Federico glared at her, but Raphael only chuckled. "Such misery!" He took her chin, studying her. "What a face you have."

"Tonight it is," agreed Federico. "After vespers bells, at the chapel doors."

"I shall think of nothing else." Raphael bowed to Federico, and turned back to the model, brush in hand. "Let us try this again," he said to his painters.

Scowling, Bee tugged her foot loose from Federico's. He

scowled back, nudging her into a spiraling stairwell. "Can you be quiet for once?" he whispered when at last they were alone.

"But tonight is so far away! What if instead—" She gasped. The tray slipped from her fingers with a clattering crash.

"What?" Federico sighed—and "Argh!" as a heavy hand fell on his shoulder.

Bee stared up slack-jawed, the crash still echoing round the stairs. "It's a—a—"

"My lord," came a voice as deep as the sea.

Federico forced himself to turn around. Above him, as tall as an alp, towered a Swiss Guard with eyes the color of ice.

Bee gulped. "It's a Swiss Guard."

"Of course," said Federico automatically. It was in fact the very Swiss Guard who had dragged him back to the palace two nights ago. Federico had hoped never to see him again.

"How fare you, my young lord?"

Federico swallowed. "I am—fine. How fare—you?" He could feel Bee vibrating beside him and prayed she would not speak.

"I, too, am fine." The huge man stared down at them, his eyes as keen as knives. "I have wondered these past days how the girl fares, and your friend. I have not seen them about."

"My friend? He is no longer here." A wave of sadness struck Federico, and he swallowed hard. "He took the girl far, far away."

The huge man pondered this. "So there is no threat of sickness to the palace?"

"Oh, no! Heavens, no."

"Miss Bother's all better," Bee chimed in, bobbing her dreadful bow. "Thank you for asking."

"I am glad to hear it." He bent down to pick up the tray. "Your words provide comfort," he said, handing it to Bee. He continued down the stairs, every step a small earthquake.

Federico exhaled.

"Wow," Bee breathed—

"My lord?" the guard rumbled from somewhere below them.

Federico jumped. "Yes?"

"His Holiness approaches. You may wish to know." The soft thunder of footsteps . . . He was gone.

"That guy is the size of an oil tanker," Bee whispered.

"His Holiness is coming?" Federico blanched. He could not meet the pope—not with Bee! He must store her somewhere till sunset. Store them both. But where?

"What is it?" Bee asked. "What's wrong?"

"I have it!" Federico hooted. "The aviary!"

"What's an avary?" Bee hurried after him.

"It's *aviary.* You'll see."

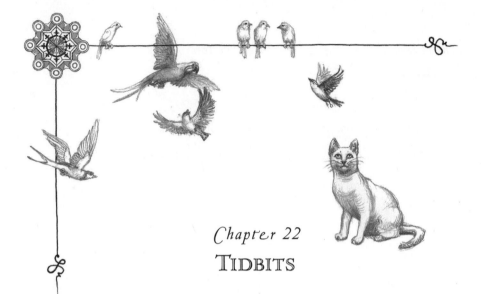

*Chapter 22*

TIDBITS

Fred must be a genius, Bee thought as she followed him through the palace. There were so many rooms to remember! And staircases. And people. Some people he bowed to, and some he nodded to, and some he pretended not to see.

They approached an open door and Fred froze. A man was talking inside. Even his voice made Bee shiver. Fred shook his head at her: *Don't move!*

Bee nodded, just the teeniest bit, to show she understood.

Fred lifted his chin and put back his shoulders. Looking straight ahead, he walked past the door. Not too fast, not too slow. Like he was walking past a bomb or the meanest table at lunch. Once at the far side, he waved for her to come.

Bee tiptoed past the doorway, not even glancing into the room. She didn't want to know.

At last they reached a steep little staircase, Fred's face lighting up as they climbed. By the top, he was almost dancing in excitement. "Behold!" He threw open the door.

A racket of birdsong hit Bee, so loud that she stumbled back. "What is this place?" she shouted.

"Do you not know an aviary? It's a palace for birds."

The room was full of songbirds in delicate birdcages. Even the windows were covered in mesh. A parrot sat squawking on a post.

Fred looked around, beaming. "Those are goldfinches," he said over the noise, pointing to a dozen fluttering creatures. "And nightingales, and parakeets from Greece. But these are my favorite." He opened a tiny curlicue door, and a little yellow bird landed on his finger. "From the Canary Islands. They are worth their weight in gold because of the beauty of their song."

"Canaries are worth their weight in gold?" Bee tried not to sound skeptical.

"Oh, yes. The King of Portugal makes great wealth from

their trade. This one was a gift to His Holiness." He stroked the little creature. "I have not visited the aviary recently, I'm afraid. I've been too busy with 'Erbert—" He caught himself. "Too busy with Juno."

Bee stared from cage to cage. "It's like a garden made out of music."

"What a nice way to phrase it." Fred smiled. Gently he returned the canary to its home. "The parrot is a gift from the Turks and can speak in Turkish, apparently. Though I don't think what it says is polite."

"Parrots." Bee nodded in sympathy. She peered between the cages, trying to see out the windows. "Is that really Rome? It's so different." The city still had red tile roofs—or already had them, she supposed. But there were so many towers! Tall and dark, looming over the streets. "What are all those towers for?"

"That's where the nobles live, naturally." Fred filled the canaries' dish from a pitcher of water. He could speak in a normal voice now. The birds were getting used to them. "You must live in a tall tower to be safe."

"I guess. It seems like an awful lot of stairs. And look how much green there is. Are those olive trees?"

"Olives, vineyards, orchards, wheat fields. How do people in your country eat? Which reminds me . . ."

Bee continued studying the city. A haze of smoke hung in the air. She could hear workmen and donkeys and chanting. But no mopeds. No sirens. No car horns. No smell of exhaust.

"Please." Fred pulled out a chair, his eyes alight. "Allow me to serve us."

Bee sat. "Thank you," she said politely. "Hey, this is backgammon." She stroked the table. "Look at that. The board is built right in."

"His Holiness and I play here sometimes." With a sweep of his arm, Fred opened a cabinet. "And behold: his secret larder! We can dine like kings—no, like popes!" He laughed, prying open a jar. "Cherries in syrup. Would you like one?" He offered her a cherry on the tip of his knife.

"Thank you." Bee popped it in her mouth. "Wow, it's like something from a fairy tale."

"Is that good?" Fred asked, worried.

"It's delicious." Wait—she had a knife, too. With some care, she speared a cherry. "Hey, I got one!" The birds seemed to twitter their support, flitting around their cages.

Fred opened another jar. "Almonds with sugar." The parrot squawked. He handed it an almond.

Bee made another stab into the jar of cherries. "Look, three in a row."

Fred laughed, lifting down a cloth-covered plate. "It's as if you've never eaten with a knife. . . . Here is parmesan cheese from the city of Parma, a favorite of His Holiness. Try it with cherry."

"I know what parmesan is." She hacked off a slice and set a cherry on top. "Wow, that's awesome. It's like salty and sweet at the same time."

"Precisely." Fred cut a perfect slice. "Tell me," he asked carefully. "What is 'Erbert's daughter like?"

"Miss Bother? She has all these drawings of Juno in her living room."

Fred's face blossomed into a smile. "Truly?"

"Herbert drew them when Juno was a kitten. They're really good. You know what's strange? Just before I came here, she said something wild."

"Wild?"

"Interesting. She said I'd make everything better." Behind Bee, even the canaries grew quiet. "She looked right at me when she said it. *I know you'll make everything better.* Her exact words."

Fred chewed. "That is interesting. We're on a quest, most definitely."

"I know, right?" She touched her neck. "How much longer till sunset?"

Fred glanced at the sun. "A few hours. What happened?" He nodded at her neck as he lifted down another jar. "Olives from Sicily. Also delicious."

"I got this scratch from climbing a tree. Which girls can do, you know." She shot him a look. "That's why Raphael needs to draw me soon. Because it's in the drawing."

"He will, he will. . . . By the way, do you play backgammon?"

Bee ate an olive. "I play with my grandfather all the time. He's really good."

"So am I. Not to boast." He pushed the jars to one side.

Bee brushed off her hands. "Me, too. Not to boast. So prepare to get clobbered." She stared at him. "There's one thing, though. About Juno."

Fred paused. "What about her?"

"You have to promise me something."

"Promise what?" His eyes tightened. "Are you threatening me?"

Bee waved at the canaries singing their love songs. The muttering parrot. The darting swallows, faster than blinks. "You have to promise never, ever, ever to let Juno into this room."

"Why not?" Fred gave her blank look.

"Because she's a cat! She'll eat every one—"

Fred's blank look dissolved into a grin.

"Hey!" Bee tried to bop him. "You know exactly what I'm talking about!"

"What?" He giggled, ducking away. "What'd I do?"

Bee lunged up, chasing him around the table, both of them laughing as loud as the birds.

*Chapter 23*

## TROUBLING REPORTS

Federico dashed out of the palace as sunset approached, his head full of giggles and his belly full of food. Bee remained behind in the aviary, chatting to the parrot and finishing off the cheese. She was, he had to admit, rather good at her variety of backgammon. But she was not nearly so skillful at the version Federico played. So they had both ended up winning, which he considered quite sporting indeed.

Federico did not go to the villa via the unfinished corridor, for he did not want to risk meeting Michelangelo returning to his studio. Instead he sprinted through the garden, leaping the shadows as swallows soared over the pine trees to celebrate the coming of dusk. The bells of Santa Rufina rang in the distance, marking the sweet little saint's upcoming feast day. What a glorious afternoon it had been. And soon, soon, he'd get to show the Sistine Chapel to Raphael and his new friend, Bee.

He hurried through the villa entrance to his room. It would be the work of a moment to retrieve the chapel key from his travel chest. He threw open the door—

"Saints above, where have you been?" shrieked Master Sniffly.

Celeste smacked Federico. "You took your mother's silver tray?"

"You missed fencing," Señor Pedro scolded. (Heavens— Señor Pedro was here as well? Federico was in trouble indeed.) "And who's this new page? We've heard troubling reports."

Federico angled toward his travel chest. "I can explain." He couldn't, but the words sounded good.

"The most shameful lad I've ever known." Again Celeste smacked him.

"The young lord can't be trusted," Master Sniffly chimed in.

"You need guarding." Señor Pedro blocked the door.

Federico dove for the chest as the blows rained down. "Forgive me, please—I quoted Virgil."

He'd blurted this out in sheer desperation, but it stopped Master Sniffly cold. "Which part?"

"What does this matter?" Señor Pedro scoffed. "'Tis training the boy needs—"

Master Sniffly drew himself upright. "Virgil is the bedrock of culture, you half-wit."

Federico dug through the chest. There—the black cloak. "Exoriare aliquis," he quoted, fumbling for the pocket. "Nostris . . . Nostris something." He snatched up the heavy iron key.

"Nowhere is safe for a Gonzaga," Señor Pedro continued. "Not without protection—"

"Nostris ex . . ." Master Sniffly prodded. "And then what?"

"Shut it," Celeste snapped at Master Sniffly. "We need to hear what this lad has been up to."

"Nostris ex . . . ossibi?" With these noble words, Federico shot out the door.

"I say, my lord!" Master Sniffly warbled. "What's the next line?"

Señor Pedro even attempted a chase, but the fighter was not built for speed.

The purpling sky hung heavy over the garden as Federico

sprinted back to the palace; a fat moon oozed over the horizon. Never had he been so naughty or so bold. To anger his tutor, his nurse, and his fencing teacher . . . He'd get thrashings for weeks.

In the aviary, the canaries had quieted with the dusk, though the swallows twittered and chattered, and the parrot was as loud as before. "You're in trouble," Bee said as soon as she saw his face.

"Yes." He did not need to say more.

In silence the two trekked through the palace, passing footmen and chamberlains, ladies in finery, musicians toting lutes. . . . Federico kept his mask smoothly in place, but Bee's face looked as worried as his heart.

Finally they reached the forecourt to the Sistine Chapel—a space nigh as big as the chapel itself, empty at this hour, and gloomy with twilight. The great carved doors filled half a wall. Music wandered through the columned windows as players somewhere struck up a song. Entwined between the notes were the church bells of vespers.

Federico peered about. Were they too late for Raphael?

"Where is he?" Bee whispered in panic.

The artist glided out of the shadows, a satchel over his

shoulder. "My lord." He bowed. He'd changed into a sleek black jerkin with handsome striped sleeves. "I was afraid you'd forgotten."

"Oh, no!" Federico waved the key, smiling brightly.

"Marvelous. Months have I waited to study this ceiling. Everyone speaks of Michelangelo's genius, but what good does that do me if he forbids me from seeing?"

Bee eyed the enormous dark doors. "What if he's still in there?"

Raphael winked at her. "The sun sets too soon for Michelangelo's liking. By which I mean there's not light enough to paint. . . . Shall we, my lord? Or are you not feeling brave?"

Federico was in fact not feeling brave in the slightest. All he could think of was Michelangelo's muscled arm with its fistful of hammers, and Michelangelo shredding drawings, his face flushed with rage. If Michelangelo learned of this tres-pass, Federico's very life might be at risk. He looked down at the key pilfered from Bramante's key ring. The architect would not be pleased.

"Fred?" Bee touched his arm. "We need to do this. Remember?"

She was right. Federico must do this, for Herbert and the promise of Juno. For the drawing.

With a deep breath, he slipped in the key. The effort required both his hands, for the lock was stiff and hefty. He turned it, throwing his whole weight into the effort.

"We enter the den of the lion." Raphael laughed, pushing the door.

"That's not reassuring!" But Bee, too, pushed.

Slowly the door opened. Somewhere in the distance a choir sang, and swallows gossiped, and sweet Santa Rufina tolled of her feast. The last rays of twilight filled the space with a magical glow; the canvas cloth stretched high above. The room's far end held an altar wrapped in shadows that looked almost like a man kneeling.

Raphael slipped into the chapel, eyes dancing. "I am already inspired."

"Wait." Federico held Bee back. The shadows seemed almost to move in the stillness. Was someone there, lurking? No—

Yes.

A phantom stepped out of the darkness. Michelangelo. "You peacock!" he roared, running at them. "Get out!" He hurled a bucket at Raphael.

"My fine man—" Raphael dodged, but too late. The bucket caught him on the forehead and he dropped like a stone.

"And you!" Michelangelo swung a tub at Federico. "A disgrace to your name." The tub hit the wall behind Federico, spraying sand everywhere.

"Master—"

"Enough!" Michelangelo ran for the door. "I am done with this city of serpents."

Bee raced to help Raphael. "This is bad. This is really, really bad."

Federico dashed after Michelangelo. "Master, it's not what you think!"

"I'll tolerate this snake pit no longer!" Michelangelo's footfalls crashed through the hallways.

Federico pounded by grubby clerks gaping like inkwells, and a message boy flattened against the wall. "Master, please stop—" Dimly he saw, or felt, a Swiss Guard, but was too panicked to pay heed.

Michelangelo threw open the heavy door to the corridor. "I'm returning to Florence!"

"I only wanted to help—" Federico gasped, chasing him.

Michelangelo unlocked the low door to his studio. "I'll

tell the world of your crimes!" With a last furious glare, he disappeared from view. The deadbolt clinked behind him.

Helplessly Federico tugged at the door. "I can explain!"

Bee galloped up. "Wait—he went in there? What do we do?"

"What are you doing here?" Federico snapped. "Michelangelo!"

"Here." Bee held up the key to the Sistine Chapel. "Take it."

"That doesn't matter! Master, open this door. Please."

"Calm down," Bee announced. "I'll fix this." She dashed back up the corridor.

Federico sprinted after her. "Where are you going?"

"Remember?" She reached the closet. "I'm making everything better." She stepped in.

"Don't—"

She was gone. Vanished as if she had never been there. Just like Herbert. Like Juno. Now he did not even have Bee.

This is what came of courage. All Federico had wanted was a friend. A pet. A quest, perhaps. But now he had nothing.

The door at the end of the corridor opened. Footsteps, coming from the palace.

Federico must hide—he needed to think! He'd made enough of a mess of this evening.

In one lunge, he opened the closet and leaped in—

And plunged from the dark Roman evening to a room filled with light. In the ceiling, candles glowed bright as the sun.

He blinked, eyes adjusting. He had stumbled into a small office with a dusty metal desk. Rusty tacks held scraps of paper to the wall. A bookcase hung from the wall—a secret bookcase, obviously, with a half-visible staircase beyond. How appropriate for Herbert.

"Bee?" he whispered. Carefully he stepped forward. The closet looked quite the same: dark wood, glass balls, strange symbols. The water sloshed in its sealed glass globe. "Juno?"

He peered under the desk. With some caution, he tugged open the drawer. Chocolate! Hastily he ripped open a package and stumbled back in disgust at the flies.

A sound drifted into the office. A shout, possibly? "Bee?" he called. His eyes fell on a thick book, the thickest he'd ever seen. It lay open on the desk—

There—his family, right on the page: GONZAGA (1328–1511). The first number he knew: 1328, the year his ancestor Luigi Gonzaga founded Mantua. The second number baffled him, though. It was as if the Gonzaga family ended. If only Federico could read what it said.

At the bottom of the page, he spotted his name. He did not like the look of *Federico Gonzaga (1500–1511)*. He did not like how GONZAGA then finished, and how the page continued with a garble of words he did not know.

Federico reached for his knife, gulping in fear. The book made it seem that he . . . that he . . .

That he was dead.

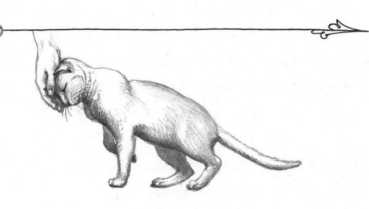

## Chapter 24
# A DIFFERENT WORLD

"I'm making everything better." That's what Bee had said, stepping away from Rome and Fred, the Sistine Chapel key in her hand. "I'm making everything better," she repeated as she stumbled out of the wardrobe into the dusty light of Herbert's office.

"Mrow?"

"Juno!" There was Juno! Sitting on the desk with her tail curled over her paws, just as Bee had left her. "I know someone who's going to be so happy to see you." See? Things were better already.

"Mrow." Juno purred, butting her hand. *Pet me.*

"Okay, okay." Bee scratched the cat's neck. "Let's get you to Fred." That's what she needed to do first. Then she and Fred could figure the rest of it out. How to get the drawing and calm down Michelangelo and help Raphael.

She frowned at the key. She should store it somewhere. Her jerkin thing didn't have pockets, but— "Look at that." It fit pretty well in her knife sheath.

Juno jumped off the desk. "Mrow."

"Hey, don't you go anywhere." She picked up the cat, heading for the wardrobe.

Juno leaped out of her arms in a smooth golden arc. "Mrow!"

"You don't want me to carry you? Then walk in." Bee held open the door.

Juno looked up at Bee. At the wardrobe. At Bee. At the half-open bookcase with stairs beyond. She turned and trotted out.

"Hey! Fred needs you." Bee bolted after her. "Wait up—" She froze.

The attic was clean. Like, weird clean. No dust on the floor. No cobwebs.

"What's going on?" she whispered.

An echo up the stairs: "Mrow. . . ."

"Juno!" Bee called, peering over the railing. She really didn't want to go downstairs. The house sounded . . . weird. Not bad, but different. Strange. "Come here, cat."

"Mrow," Juno called, fainter.

Bee crept down the steps. "Juno, this is really irritating." She had better things to do right now than chase a cat who wasn't even hers. She reached the second floor hallway. "Hey, Juno—" She looked around. "What?"

The bedroom door stood open—the bedroom with dark furniture and the painting of young Miss Bother . . . But there wasn't any furniture in the room. It was perfectly swept. Not a speck.

"Hello?" Bee's voice echoed like in a horror movie. She tiptoed backward, feeling for the railing.

"Mrow," Juno yowled from below.

Bee sprinted down the stairs.

The first floor was even worse. The living room was bare. Just a battered wood floor.

Bee dashed into the dining room. "Miss Bother?" But the dining room was empty, too. No table or envelopes or bed. No curtains. No art—

"Excuse me*!*"

"Aah*!*" Bee screamed.

A woman stepped out of the kitchen, her heels tapping. She carried a clipboard like it was attached to her arm. "What are you doing here?" She eyed Bee's hose.

Bee bent over, trying to breathe. "You gave me a heart attack. . . . Who are you?"

A guy in a plaid jacket wandered into the front hall. "That cat door needs to be sealed," he told the woman. "I don't want strays in the house." He frowned at Bee. "Who's that?"

Bee stared at the wall above the dining room fireplace. There wasn't a mark. Not a nail. Like nothing hung there, ever.

Like Raphael's drawing had never existed.

The woman yanked open the front door. "I don't know who you are or how you got in this house, but you have to leave."

Bee backed up. "I—I just need my cat. . . ."

"The cat left." The guy shifted, blocking the kitchen.

"Yeah—I—" Bee bit her lip. "I need—" She couldn't think!

The guy stepped toward her. "You need to exit this building."

"Yeah. Gotcha." Bee took another step—and spun. As fast as she could, she fled up the stairs.

"Hey, kid! Get back here!"

Bee pounded to the landing—the second floor—the third. She hurled herself into Herbert's office. With all her strength, she slammed the bookcase closed—

"Aah!" she screamed. "What are you doing here?"

Fred stood in the office, knife in hand. Candy wrappers covered the floor, and flies. The encyclopedia stood open on the desk. "I am dead."

"No, you're not. Listen, I found Juno but there's this huge enormous problem—"

"Read it to me." Dully Fred gestured at the encyclopedia.

"—with Miss Bother. . . . Are you okay?"

"Read it." Fred stabbed the page. He looked gray.

Bee squinted. "It says—I'll just translate—*following the death of both Federico Gonzaga and Michelangelo in 1511*—" Her head shot up. "This is wrong. Michelangelo lived to be eighty-something."

"What does it say?"

"Moo told me. He was, like, eighty-five. . . ." She bent back over the book. "So blah blah blah 1511, *Pope Julius II*

201

*claimed Mantua, ending the family line."* She swallowed. "And that's it."

"Why does it say I'm dead? I'm not dead. I am here."

"I know, right?" Bee flipped to the next bookmark. "MENNONITE, MEXICO . . . MICHELANGELO. Huh." The entry had been longer before. Uh-oh.

"What is it? Tell me."

"Let me just read the end, okay? Um, *in July 1511, Michelangelo was involved in the disappearance and presumed death of young Federico Gonzaga—*" She looked up. "Meaning people think something but they're not sure—"

"I know the word 'presumed.'"

"Yeah. Okay. *Michelangelo fled to Florence, where he died"*— she took a deep breath—*"two weeks later."*

"What else?"

"*Bramante immediately ordered the ceiling of the Sistine Chapel painted over. No images remain."* Bee felt like she'd been punched in the stomach. "This is wrong. This has to be wrong. Because you're alive, right? And Michelangelo isn't in Florence."

"Yes, he is." Fred's voice sounded like the end of the world. "He's going there now."

"Um, so? This is just a book. It doesn't *know* what happened—"

"I am dead." Fred stepped into the wardrobe. "'Erbert is dead. Michelangelo will be dead soon."

Bee grabbed for the wardrobe door. "Wait—what about Juno? We need to—"

Fred slammed the door shut.

Bee yanked it open. The wardrobe was empty. Desperately she peered around the office. The phone! She sprang for it, knocking away candy wrappers. "Pick up, Mom," she begged, dialing.

"You've reached Miriam Bliss. Please leave a message."

"Hi, Mom. I'm at Miss Bother's and I, um, I need to find Juno and Fred's really upset and the drawing is gone. . . ." The message didn't make sense even to her. "Never mind. I'll call Moo." Quickly she dialed. A click. "Hi, Moo, I've got this thing going on and I really need your help—"

A lady's voice came on the line. A robot lady. "We're sorry," the robot announced, "but this number is not in service. Please check your number and try again."

Bee hung up the phone.

"It's okay," she whispered. "You've got this. Don't freak."

She dialed again.

"We're sorry but this number is not in service."

Slowly Bee hung up. Where was Moo? "Where are you?" Bee asked the air. She stared at the dusty yellow note cards. NO TIME PASSES. HOW DOES THE CAT MOVE? The 1942 calendar. A blank spot on the wall. Something should be in that blank spot. Bee couldn't remember what, though, because her brain was too busy freaking.

# PART IV

# THE UNTANGLING

## Chapter 25
## AN HOUR'S HEAD START

Federico stepped out of the closet holding his breath. If this was his last bit of air, he wanted to save it. His tread echoed in the dark corridor, the scratch of grit as loud as a scream. Moonlight fell like scars across the floor. The breeze carried wood smoke and orange blossoms, incense and pee. Bells tolled somewhere, the pealing almost visible in the thick air: Santo Spirito. Santa Rufina.

Federico stood listening, every nerve alert. He was—it seemed—still alive.

Santo Spirito faded to silence, but Santa Rufina continued her sweet tolling. . . . Ah, the feast day. Federico had been gone two hours at most. As Herbert predicted, the closet had returned him at midnight.

He straightened his cloak—his sky-blue cloak with the cream silk detail—and adjusted his cap trimmed in pearls. Never again, he vowed, would he disobey. He'd not sneak from his room, nor straggle through Latin, nor better His Holiness at backgammon. . . .

His Holiness.

Federico's joy vanished. Michelangelo had fled Rome. He was the pope's favorite artist, however the two men might argue. When His Holiness discovered Michelangelo gone, Federico's life would be as good as over. Federico had stolen the key to the chapel and opened the chapel door. Palace gossips would tell the pope as much—social climbers desperate to smirk that the Gonzaga could not be trusted, that Federico's father must be replaced and the castle given to someone more deserving. . . .

A sob bubbled in Federico's chest. He was going to perish, exactly as Herbert's book said. The Gonzaga family would end, due to him.

The bells of Santa Rufina tolled. Between each note, silence swelled. Silence, and a rustle.

Federico leaped to attention, knife in hand.

Bee stumbled out of the closet already jabbering.

Federico sheathed his knife. "Bee," he said dully. "Hello."

"Hey, you're not dead. Told you."

"But I am. When His Holiness learns that Michelangelo has left, he'll end the Gonzaga."

But Bee was too busy chattering to listen—something about family. His sisters in Mantua might soon be dead, too. At the very least, dishonored.

Federico's grief swelled into rage. "This is all your fault!" he yelled, jabbing at her jerkin—*his* jerkin! "If you hadn't shown up with your stupid ideas—"

It was no use. Why waste breath fighting girls? Federico must find peace elsewhere. Seething, he marched away.

"Where are you going?" Bee called. "Back to your fancy-shmancy bedroom?"

He was too angry to reply.

"What, you're going to chase Michelangelo?"

"A Gonzaga does not chase—" He bit his tongue. He had no interest in Bee, nor Michelangelo; not even Juno. His sole focus—the most important concern in the world—was his family.

How dare Bee suggest he chase Michelangelo like a puppy after a rabbit. He could not leave the palace, for one thing. Only bandits and murderers traveled the city this late, and messengers. Soldiers. He shuddered, remembering his mortifying encounter with the Swiss Guard. Besides, Michelangelo was doubtless halfway to the Florence border. Catching him would require the fastest horse in Rome. An Arabian, bred for distance and speed. Federico knew of such a creature, yes, but she belonged to the ambassador of Venice, for official business. By messengers.

Federico was not a messenger—just look at his cloak, and his cap trimmed with pearls. To play the part of a messenger would mean hiding everything that gave him meaning. He'd have to erase himself in the hope—the faint hope—of somehow convincing Michelangelo to return to Rome. Ridiculous.

But.

But what choice did he have? He could retreat to his bedroom, to Celeste and Señor Pedro and Master Sniffly, but that would end badly.

He could run away—

Greater shame still.

He could plead with His Holiness. Which would not work.

Or it might, but His Holiness would make it a spectacle, and force Federico to crawl on his knees before the whole city, begging forgiveness. His Holiness enjoyed such displays. Federico was a hostage, after all. It would be a good message to convey to the many enemies of the pope.

Federico removed his cap, stroking the pearls. How they shone in the moonlight. Two hundred ducats they were worth, easily. A workman toiled years to earn so much.

To catch Michelangelo, he would need a horse and a squadron's worth of bravery. Courage he could muster. He was a warrior, after all, or would be; he was almost the age of a man. A fast horse, however, required wealth. Wealth, and cunning . . .

Slowly at first, Federico began to run. Through the long corridor, all the way to its end. Through the vast shadowy garden. Through the maze of the stables to the room of the saddler. God willing, the man slept lightly. He tapped at the door. "Excuse me. It is late for good men, but I must speak."

It was late for good men, yes. But the saddler was not good.

The door cracked open. The saddler squinted at Federico, a smile tugging at the scar on his cheek. "The little troublemaker."

Federico had no time to take offense. "I need a horse. Please."

The saddler leaned on the doorframe. "The sculptor was here. Michelangelo. That's what he called you. 'Federico, the trouble-maker,' he said, before he rode off. Ordered me to repeat it."

"Ah." Federico kept his face stony. "Fascinating." He took a deep breath. "Master Saddler, you are—we both know—a man of business."

The saddler smirked. "That I am."

He looked the saddler in the eye. "I need the fastest horse in this stable."

"That's quite a request." The saddler stroked his scar. "The Venetian ambassador has a mare that can outrun the wind. But she's not mine to sell."

"Certainly she's not yours to sell." Federico slipped off his cloak—the sky-colored cloak lined with silk. "I do not need to *buy* a horse." He shook it, and the silk shimmered like a warm private sea. The fabric alone cost a hundred ducats. "I need to borrow one for several hours. Nothing more."

The saddler stared at the gleaming fabric. "She's not been ridden for days. But the risk I take . . ." His eyes darted to Federico.

Federico removed his blue silk cap. Six years of wages, just for the pearls. "A risk we both take."

The saddler's eyes narrowed. "Michelangelo was right about you. Quite the little rule breaker."

Federico shrugged. "A gentleman does not break rules. You taught me that." He tossed the cap to the saddler. "A gentleman learns how to bend them."

The saddler caught it. Of course he did. What sort of man drops six years of wages on the floor of a stable?

Federico held out the cloak. "And a saddle. Please."

Not fifteen minutes later, Federico was trotting into the city on a black mare named Bathsheba, the fastest horse in all of Rome. He rode in his jerkin, bare sleeved and bareheaded, his rings tucked in a pocket, for the slightest flash of gold would expose him. Knife in hand, he inspected every shadow as the mare's hoofbeats thumped the dirt. Men would kill for a horse such as this. Men would kill their own brothers, and for good reason. Federico had been riding horses since before he could walk; he knew horses like his mother knew art. But never had he met a horse like Bathsheba.

He slowed the mare as they approached the city gates. "I am a messenger," he cried. "Open, please." *I must retrieve*

*Michelangelo,* he wanted to add—but did not.

"For whom do you ride?" called a voice from the tower.

"For His Holiness." These were, after all, the pope's men. "And for Venice," in case they knew the mare.

He could not see the men in the darkness. Perhaps the gates never opened so late. Perhaps a messenger was too lowly to heed.

In one motion he dismounted, reins in his left hand, knife in his right. "There is no time!" he called, desperation lacing his words.

A gate man in armored breastplate stepped from the shadows. "You're small for a messenger." He lounged against a narrow door built into the wall—a sally port, for just such moments when a single soul needed to leave.

"So they tell me," Federico said humbly. *I must catch Michelangelo!* he wanted to scream.

Bathsheba huffed in irritation at the delay. Federico held the knife behind his back, shifting his grip. He did not want to attack this man, but Señor Pedro had taught him ways to pierce armor.

"Clear," the voice called down, finally.

With a shrug, the gate man lifted the sally port's crossbar.

Reins in hand, Federico brushed past. "Thank you."

"Another cup of grain and she wouldn't make it." The gate man laughed. But Federico did not reply, for already he was swinging himself into the saddle—

And already Bathsheba was running. She reached full gallop before he even sat down, her hoofs pounding over the drawbridge. A lesser horseman would have ended up in the ditch. As it was, Federico clutched her mane for dear life. Oh, she was fast. She let out one triumphant snort and shook her ears and she flew.

The men behind him cheered, but Federico could not hear their words for the thunder of hoofbeats. He clung like a flea, his cheek pressed to Bathsheba's neck. Her mane whipped his face; the wind clawed tears from his eyes. The road lay before them, every stone bright in the moonlight. "Run, Bathsheba," he whispered. "Find him."

## Chapter 26

# EVERYTHING IS WORSE

Bee tumbled through the wardrobe back into Rome. She didn't have a choice. Those two people were going to kick her out of Miss Bother's house!

She'd heard them coming up the stairs outside Herbert's office. "She's got to be here somewhere," the woman said, her heels tapping.

"Why are there still books in the bookcase?" the guy asked—the guy in that ugly plaid jacket. "All this junk is supposed to be gone. . . . Whoa, what's that?"

Bee stared in horror as the bookcase shifted. She hadn't shut it completely.

"Interesting," the woman murmured. "I don't think it's attached to the wall." Bee watched in terror as red fingernails came into view. "Is there a room back here—?"

Bee edged away, groping for somewhere to hide—and hurled herself through the wardrobe . . . into the palace corridor. "Fred!" she cried, catching sight of him. "It's so terrible—there are these people in Miss Bother's house but she's not there and her stuff isn't either, and Moo's phone isn't working which is totally awful, and I tried to get Juno but she ran away—"

Fred stared at her. "Bee. Hello."

"Hey, you're not dead." Obviously the encyclopedia was wrong. "Told you."

"But I am. . . ."

Bee stared at the wardrobe. What if those people were in Herbert's office right now? Why was the house so empty? "I think something happened to Miss Bother. I don't know how because I wasn't gone at all because no time passes and Juno was sitting in the exact same place—Hello, Fred? Herbert's daughter? His family? Don't you care?"

Without warning, Fred poked her in the chest. "This is all your fault!" he hissed.

Bee slapped his hand away. "What are you talking about?

This is a quest, remember? For both of us. We've got to make everything better."

"We do not! It is not *my* quest!" With a snarl of fury, Fred stomped away.

"Where are you going?" she called, as sarcastically as she could. "Back to your fancy-shmancy bedroom?"

He didn't answer. His cloak rippled in the moonlight.

"What, you're going to chase Michelangelo?"

He didn't flinch. Even his footsteps sounded mad.

"Don't you care about Juno?" Her words echoed down the corridor. "You're not the boss of me, you know."

He paused in a patch of moonlight.

"Fred?"

But it was like he didn't even hear. Instead he took off running, his feet a fast-fading drumbeat.

What was she supposed to do now? *I should call Moo,* she thought automatically, glancing at the wardrobe. Moo would know—

But Moo's phone didn't work.

Bee stared at the wardrobe with its eight glass balls. What had happened to Miss Bother? And why was Fred being such a jerk? This wasn't Bee's fault. If anything, it was Fred's fault, because now she was crying. This whole thing was so dumb! It couldn't get any worse—

*Thud.* The door to the palace closed.

Bee's heart dropped to the floor.

"Where is he?" a deep voice growled. Footsteps approached. "Where is the young lord?" The Swiss Guard! The Swiss Guard the size of an oil tanker, his face dark under his helmet. His sword alone was bigger than Bee.

Bee jerked her chin down the corridor. "He went that way." She eased herself toward the wardrobe—

The guard grabbed her by the back of the neck. "He is not in the villa. I checked." He was almost lifting her off her feet. "His people are insane with worry."

"I mean—" Bee pulled at her collar. "I mean he wasn't there earlier. He went there just now."

The guard was quiet. So quiet that Bee could hear bells in the distance, and music.

She squirmed. "Um, we had a fight."

The guard turned her face, studying her in the moonlight. "Two nights ago, I found his lordship wandering the city with some poppycock tale about Raphael. Tonight, Raphael had a poppycock tale about him."

"Yeah." Bee gulped. "It's a long story."

"Why was he sprinting through the garden this afternoon like an errand boy?"

"Because . . ." Bee couldn't think! And the guard's eyes were so angry—like white fire. "Um, remember when you asked about the girl? Miss Bother?"

"You said"—his voice harsh—"that she was better."

"She was! But it's different now. It's really hard to explain." The wardrobe was only three steps away. If she could just twist free, she'd jump in—

The guard pushed her up the corridor. "Enough."

"You can't do this—I'm trying to explain—" She scrabbled at his arm, her fingers slipping on the velvet. "Fred!" she screamed.

"Hush," the guard ordered, opening the door to the palace. "You'll wake people."

This was not good. This was really, really not good. "Seriously, what do you want to know?" Bee babbled as he marched her through the dark rooms. "It's the wardrobe, okay? It was made by da Vinci—there's a cat—"

"Silence." He half-pushed, half-carried her down a narrow staircase. A second staircase. Bee's hose-shoes slipped; she had to grab at the wall. The guard's hand never moved from her neck.

A third staircase, so dark Bee could see only blackness. The air pressed at her face like a wet towel, reeking of old meat and garlic and poo. "Um, excuse me," she said, as politely as she could. "I'm just wondering where we are going. Please. If you wanted to tell me—"

"His lordship is only a boy."

"Me, too!" Bee exclaimed quickly. But that didn't seem to help.

A lantern flickered in the passage ahead, lighting the rough walls. A man paced—another Swiss Guard, helmet under his arm, rubbing his short hair.

"My duty is to His Holiness," the huge guard intoned, opening a plain wooden door. He looked down at Bee. "But I do not want to see harm befall him."

"Franz!" The second guard hurried over. "The young lord has left the city. I saw it myself."

The huge guard—Franz?—shook Bee. "What is this?" He leaned close, scowling. "Tell me."

"I don't know. I don't know anything!" Bee winced back a sob.

Franz glared at her. "Useless," he spat, tossing her through the door. A slam. Footsteps stomped off.

Bee stumbled, gasping for breath.

She rubbed her neck, peering around. She was in a tiny cell that stank of leather and sweat. Moonlight lit a narrow bed heaped with blankets, and a finely carved shelf. "I didn't know," she whispered. "I thought Fred was going back to his room." She wiped her nose. "Moo? Mom? I need help."

A creak—a movement.

Across the room, the blankets shifted.

Screaming, Bee hurled herself at the door.

"Oh, sad one," a voice murmured. "What have you done?"

## Chapter 27

## THE RIDE

And now Federico was outside Rome, far beyond the city walls, pounding across the wild Roman countryside. Bathsheba's hoofs beat a steady rhythm that devoured the miles; her coat showed not a bead of sweat. A horse should not run too long, Federico knew, for like a person it will tire. A soldier who walked his horse journeyed farther in the end, and arrived with both of them fresh. So Federico let Bathsheba gallop away the staleness of the stable, then slowed her to a trot. "Do not fret, pretty girl." He patted her neck. "You shall run again soon."

In the distance behind them rose the towers of Rome,

silhouetted against the mountains and the star-filled sky. Moonlight lit the highway so empty and flat, the wheat fields, the few rough huts; the breeze smelled of manure and swamp. How naked Federico felt without cap or cloak—but tonight he was a messenger, not a lord. Fine clothes would only mark him as someone important, someone worth robbing or holding for ransom. Men of power traveled this highway in daylight, with guards and hired soldiers. A humble messenger, however, would not attract attention at this late hour. . . .

Or would he?

Their first misfortune came as they climbed a hill. Aware of the distance they must ride, Federico had dismounted. *All weight is heavy,* Señor Pedro often scolded. It felt good to stretch his legs, though pebbles poked at his thin soles. He kept an eye on the road as he walked, reins in hand, Bathsheba's pretty head turning this way and that.

Her ears pricked forward.

"What is it?" Federico clambered into the saddle. From horseback he'd have a much better view. No sooner was he seated, however, than the bushes erupted. Men lunged at him, and a snarling dog the size of a mastiff—

Bathsheba leaped forward, kicking the dog. "Go!" screamed

Federico, knife drawn, as the giant dog snapped at her hoofs. Four men ran toward them, swinging cudgels. Their hats covered their faces with shadow. Or perhaps they wore masks. Or perhaps they were demons. . . .

"No!" he screamed, at the bandits and the dog and fate itself.

Bathsheba shot away, the bandits in her dust. The dog kept pace till she kicked it again, and it rolled howling into the ditch.

Federico risked a backward glance as he crouched in the saddle, the wind whipping his hair. "Ha!" he shouted, waving his knife. What a triumph. He wished his parents could see him. And Bee. And Herbert.

Federico settled into the saddle, grinning. "Good girl." How brave they'd both been.

Eventually the mare slowed to a rocking canter that ate through the miles. Federico never stopped scanning the road, the bushes, the fields. He held his knife tight when they passed overgrowth, or vineyards knotted with shadow. Kidnapping no longer worried him. Bandits such as those four men would not kidnap a solitary messenger. They'd kill him for the horse. Had Michelangelo encountered bandits?

Though even bandits would be mad to take on Michelangelo, who had muscles and hammers and rage.

At long last Federico caught sight of a lantern. He sighed in relief: a post inn for travelers. A stable boy ran out as he trotted into the courtyard. "Bathsheba," the boy cried. He took her reins, barely glancing at the rider.

Federico slipped from the saddle. At that moment the splash of the horse trough sounded sweeter than honey. "Has a man passed recently?" he asked, gulping down water. Beside him, Bathsheba drank deep. "He has an odd neck." Federico cocked his head to demonstrate.

The stable boy nodded. "He smelled something terrible. And he said terrible things about Mantua."

"How dare you—" Federico caught himself. "Might my horse have some grain?" he asked politely, tugging Bathsheba away from the trough. She'd get colic if she drank too much. As she ate, he listened to the stable boy describe how the smelly man had refused to change horses, so desperate had he been to leave the pope's country. "Then I must hurry, too," Federico said grimly, leading Bathsheba back to the road.

Though he yearned to gallop, Federico walked Bathsheba some distance, letting the water and grain settle within her.

At least, he comforted himself, he could play a messenger. The stable boy proved that.

The terrain was rougher now, with long stretches of climb-ing. The moon crept its way across the heavens; morning, it seemed, would never come. Federico walked the hills and rode Bathsheba at a slow pace on the downslopes, fearful she might stumble. Otherwise they trotted, and only sometimes cantered when one or the other could not stand the slowness of the pace.

Trouble returned during a climb. Federico walked silently, knife in hand, listening for any rustle. Bathsheba set each hoof with purpose, ears pricked. At the sound of hoofbeats, they both started, and Federico was in the saddle before his next breath.

Bathsheba ran, her neck long, but she was not fresh, and the riders were soon upon them. A bandit, bearded and scarred, pounded next to Federico, his horse matching Bathsheba stride for stride. He grabbed for her reins—

Federico stabbed at him, slashing the bandit's gloved hand. Again he stabbed—

Cursing, the bandit let go. But Federico had not a moment of rest, for a second outlaw appeared on his left—

Galloping with all her might, Bathsheba bit at the other

horse, screaming like the fighter she was. Federico caught the bandit's reins with his knife blade, and with a fierce tug sliced them through. The rider fell back at once.

Bent low on Bathsheba, Federico struggled to hear over her pounding hoofs and the pounding of his heart. Did more men follow? He did not have the courage to look back.

But if bandits did trail them, they lacked Bathsheba's spirit. On she flew, tension easing; her hoofs now sounded out rhythms instead of alarms. "You are worth your weight in silver," Federico whispered, stroking her neck.

By now Federico's bottom was so sore that he welcomed walking on foot. Bathsheba lagged, her head low. Perhaps they'd never catch Michelangelo. Perhaps Federico was fated to die after all, the last of the Gonzaga.

Ahead rose a hilltop marked by lights. An enemy, or an inn? Federico could not be sure. It took effort to climb into Bathsheba's saddle, for exhaustion filled his bones. Exhaustion and fear.

Cautiously he rode forward.

"Halt!" bawled a voice. "Halt in the name of Florence."

Federico almost collapsed with relief. He had reached the border. Dismounting, he did his best not to fall. "I seek a man who rode through here—"

"Michelangelo, you mean?" A stable man approached, lantern high. "You look a right beggar, mate."

Federico held out the reins. "Might you care for her, please?"

The stableman took the reins with a nod. "You know you're bleeding?"

Federico glanced down. His sleeve was slashed and bloody. "That's from a bandit, I think."

"You're tougher than you look." The stable man nodded to the inn. "He's there. Stay upwind."

Federico limped across the courtyard. The eastern horizon held the promise of dawn.

With a deep breath, he opened the door.

The inn consisted of a low room with a floor that looked older than time. Embers glowed in the hearth, barely lighting the rough tables and stools. Michelangelo sat alone, head cocked as always. "Hmph. Federico. Come to beg forgiveness?"

Federico eased himself into a chair. Somewhere close, bread was baking. "Yes. Forgive me. I beg you."

Michelangelo dunked a crust into a chipped bowl of water. "Never."

"Please. If you do not return to Rome, my family will suffer."

A shrug. "How is that my problem?"

"But Mantua—my country—"

"Yes. Your country. Not mine." Michelangelo swept the crumbs into one brawny hand and dumped them into his mouth. "You see this? The greatest artist in Rome, and I eat like a prisoner."

Federico sighed. He had heard too many times about Michelangelo's so-called poverty. "You have money, Master. You own a village."

"I am not respected. I am a genius, and people"—he glared at Federico—"sneak behind my back."

Federico dropped his head. "Yes. But—"

"Upstarts copy me. They mock." Michelangelo stood, head tilted, pushing away the bowl. "But no more."

"Master, you cannot." Federico's voice rose in desperation. "I need you! The dishonor—"

"Your dishonor." Michelangelo strode across the room. "I am in my country now." His eyes flicked across Federico's filthy breeches and bloody sleeve. "I don't have to listen to beggars." He slammed the door as he left.

## Chapter 28
# THE CLIMB

Trapped in a moonlit cell in the depths of the palace, Bee stared in horror at the shifting lump of blankets. "Wha—?" she gasped, groping for the door.

Again the thing moved, and swung its legs to the floor, and became a man in a black shirt with striped sleeves. And that voice: *What have you done?* She knew that voice. Raphael.

"Wait—what?" Bee tried to keep her own voice from shaking. "Why are you in jail?"

"Jail?" Raphael chuckled, straightening his sleeves. "Silly child, we're in the barracks of the Swiss Guards. They're quite fond of me here."

"But why is that guard so mad at Fred—I mean, Sir Federico?"

"Franz? Quite the opposite. If His Holiness lost his young hostage. . . ." Carefully he stood, peering into a mirror propped on the shelf. "Saints above. At least I won't have a scar." He grimaced, testing his bruised forehead. "So much for seeing the Sistine Chapel."

"Wait—" But that was the whole point! "But you still need to draw me."

Raphael dabbed at the bruise. "Too bad it's locked."

"It's locked?" Suddenly Bee's chest didn't feel quite so tight.

"So I'm afraid we haven't a deal. Now be a dear and find me my cap. Black, tasteful, small . . . There it is."

"So if you could get into the chapel," Bee asked slowly, "you would draw me?"

Raphael set a satchel across his chest. "I've got the sketch-book right here. If only our plan had worked." He arranged his cap in the mirror. "I must thank Franz for being such a good host. . . ." His voice died as he looked down at the key in Bee's hand.

"We still have time," she whispered. That space over Miss

Bother's fireplace—they still had time, right? Maybe?

Raphael stared at the key, tapping his chin in thought.

"Michelangelo has gone to Florence." Bee must convince this man! "Don't you want to see the greatest art in the world?"

Raphael stiffened. "That's a little strong."

He was listening, though. He was interested. "It's what my mom says." Bee stuck her head out the door. "Excuse me? We need to borrow this lantern." She turned back to Raphael. "Please? It's an emergency."

"The greatest art in the world?" Raphael sniffed. But he followed her into the hall.

Together they trotted up the narrow staircase and the second and the third, Bee so excited that she wanted to run. Behind her, Raphael's eyes gleamed. For all his pooh-poohing, he looked almost hungry. They trekked through dark rooms crowded with ladders, though empty echoing hallways as Bee's borrowed lantern caught the gold-painted details. . . . Finally they reached the forecourt of the Sistine Chapel with its doors half the size of the wall. Bee forced the key into the lock.

Raphael laid his hands over hers. "He's truly gone?"

She nodded.

Raphael grinned, licking his lips. Together they pushed open the door.

The great chapel lay before them, the floor gliding silently into darkness. Moonlight gleamed down from high windows. The enormous canvas stretched above their heads, rustling in the breath of night. Beyond it rose the other half of the ceiling, patient and gray.

Bee stepped across the threshold, the shadows drinking her footsteps. Her eyes went to the blank part of the ceiling. That's what the whole thing used to look like. That's what it'd look like again if—

*Don't think that,* she told herself. "Come on."

She climbed the ladder hand over hand, up and up and up. Raphael followed, as silent as a cat. More silent, because he didn't mrow. Where, she wondered, was Juno now?

*Don't think that.*

From the top of the ladder she could barely see the floor. There wasn't even a railing! The ceiling curved over her head, ghostly in the lantern light. The scaffolding rose with it like bleachers in a gym. Beneath Bee's feet, the planks creaked. But the scaffolding was strong—it'd been built to hold Michelangelo plus his assistants. Moo probably knew all their names.

Moo would love this. She would love it so much.

Raphael eased his way onto the scaffolding, his head turning as he tried to take it all in. Below them, the canvas whispered and sighed.

Bee pointed to the top of the ceiling. "That's Adam and Eve. That's my mom's favorite part."

"May I?" Raphael asked, taking the lantern. He stepped around a wooden pulley, heading for the nearest wall.

Raphael might not be interested in Adam, but Bee was. How could she not be? She'd had to look at him so many times. She couldn't wait to see him close. Up she climbed past a coil of rope, a stack of chisels, heading to the top.

*Do you see his energy?* Moo had asked the Japanese tourists. *Do you feel it?* She'd positioned Bee's arms to demonstrate Adam reaching for the apple. *Join in!* she'd told the tourists. And they had, laughing as they felt the energy of Adam and the energy of Moo. Bee had laughed, too. She'd been embarrassed, sure. But she'd also been happy.

A board squeaked: Raphael. He lifted the lantern to look at the image of a man in a robe, his arm crossed over his chest.

Raphael turned his own body, imitating the pose. Letting his hand droop midair . . .

Most artists, Moo explained, painted the Garden of Eden like it was all Eve's fault. Like Eve tricked Adam. A woman tricking a man. But not Michelangelo. For Michelangelo, sin was just as much Adam's fault.

Raphael strolled along the scaffolding, the lantern light circling him like a halo. He examined a woman rocking a baby, her shoulder turned protectively, her head bent.

Bee reached the top of the scaffolding, so close that she almost could touch Adam. Moo always got mad when people said Michelangelo lay on his back to paint. *He stood!* she'd say, stretching her arm up, her head tilted. Now Bee stretched, too. How many people in the history of the world got to see Adam from four feet away? Got to see him reach for the apple?

How come Moo's phone didn't work?

Raphael was looking at a young woman holding a scroll, the lantern shifting as he breathed. Bee knew that figure, too. Moo had it on a poster over her desk. The woman was a prophet from Ancient Greece. Bee loved how strong she looked, and how beautiful. But the woman was worried. She really did see the future—you could tell. How would she warn everyone? What would she say?

What had happened to Moo?

Slowly Raphael lowered the lantern.

Above Bee's head, the scene continued as an angel banished Adam and Eve from Eden. Adam was turning his face away— he couldn't even look at the garden. *I'm sorry,* he seemed to be saying. *I screwed up. I know I was wrong.*

The light swayed as Raphael fell to his knees.

If Michelangelo died, all these pictures would be covered.

*We're sorry but this number is not in service.*

If Michelangelo died, then he'd never be old. So Moo would never be in Rome researching him. So she would never meet Mom.

A raw gasp broke the silence: Raphael, crying.

If Moo didn't meet Mom, they wouldn't get married.

If Mom and Moo didn't get married, they'd never have Bee.

*You'll make everything better,* Miss Bother had said, back when Miss Bother at least had a drawing, and a house.

Bee, though . . . Bee had made everything worse.

## Chapter 29

## EVERY GESTURE MATTERS

Federico sat in the inn, head in hands. He had failed. Michelangelo was again on his way to the city of Florence. Even now Federico could hear him bellowing for a mount.

Federico's life was as good as over. What would become of the Gonzaga? *Ending the family line*—that's what Herbert's book said. His Holiness would claim Mantua and the Gonzaga castle, his mother's art collection, his father's title if not his head. . . . Federico could not bear to think of their faces, and their disappointment. Already the shame burned like fire.

His arm hurt. Back when he was a child, before this night began, Federico would have thrilled at such a wound. He'd have boasted to Señor Pedro and let Celeste pamper him. Now, however, he didn't care enough even to pull back his sleeve.

Dully he thought of Juno, wherever she was. All he'd wanted was a friend. Now look.

Behind him, a door opened. Not Michelangelo returning to torment him—that'd be too fortunate. "'Scuse me, sir, can I get you anything?"

"No." Federico pushed his hair from his eyes. "But thank you."

The voice belonged to a girl in a blouse dusted with flour. The baker's girl, trailing the warm scent of bread. "'Tis no problem, sir."

Federico looked at his shirt splattered with blood, his grimy hands. His jerkin was so dirty that the embroidery could no longer be seen. He lacked a cap. *A right beggar*, the soldier called him. *I don't listen to beggars*, Michelangelo had sneered. "You called me sir," he murmured, almost to himself. Never in his life had he looked less like a gentleman.

"I calls everyone sir, sir. Makes them feel special." She bobbed a curtsy as terrible as one of Bee's bows. It was the sort of mistake Bee would make, calling a messenger sir.

Federico dropped his head. It didn't matter. It didn't matter how this girl addressed commoners or noblemen. He was going to end up as a sentence in a book that no one would read. In the future men paid no attention to rank or to birth-right. Herbert had adopted a beggar! Bee did not even know the family name Gonzaga. She cared only about artists.

His head came up.

She cared only about artists . . . and their art.

"Excuse me," he called. "What if someone were actually special?"

"I wouldn't know, sir." Nervously the baker's girl glanced toward her kitchen, wiping her hands on her apron.

Federico stood. Hope fluttered in his chest like a songbird. "What if someone truly special came here? What if you had to serve the King of France?"

The girl looked at the low beams, the rough floor. "I'm not—I don't know—he'd never—"

"But say he did." Federico pulled a ring from his pocket and pressed it into her hand. "I need a feast. Can you do that? I need your best food, I need candles, I need tablecloths—" He swept his arm wide. "I need magnificence."

"The King of France?" She looked dazed. "We've got nothing prepared."

"You must." A kitchen always had something, especially at an inn. "Cheese, salami—whatever's in your larder. Fruit. Nuts. Bread." He flapped at her. "Go!"

"The bread needs cooling, sir—"

"No, it doesn't." Federico ran outside. "Master!" What if Michelangelo had already left? His plan would be for nothing.

But Michelangelo had not left; he was far too bad-tempered for that. Instead he stood in the stable yard brandishing a coin. "This is good money. Now take it!"

"'Tis not the coin of Florence," the stable man bellowed back.

"Master!" Federico ran between them. "Master, please come back in."

"Why?" Michelangelo snapped. "Why should I listen to a troublemaker?"

Federico handed the stable man a ring—a gold band set with amber from the Baltic Sea. "That little mare? Please treat her like the queen that she is." He turned to Michelangelo. "Come, Master. There's warm bread."

"I don't care about bread."

Federico nudged him forward. "I have a story to tell you. You'll like it."

"I won't," declared Michelangelo, scowling.

"It's a true story. About you."

Michelangelo feigned disinterest. "Is it gossip?"

"Quite the opposite. It's a prophecy." He took Michelangelo's arm. It was like gripping an oak tree. "Please?"

"Prophecy. Hmph." But Michelangelo allowed Federico to coax him inside.

Candles now lit the room. A tray of cheeses and sausages sat on the table, and a pitcher of wine, and grapes. The baker's girl was putting out two bowls as they entered. "It's yesterday's stew," she stammered, "for the stable men—"

"It smells of heaven," Federico assured her, guiding Michelangelo to the chair. He himself would take a stool. Every gesture mattered.

Michelangelo sniffed at the stew. "Is there a fork?" Of course he'd ask for a fork, the braggart. Federico was so hungry that he'd lap at the bowl like a dog.

"Here, sir," the girl answered. "I'll get the bread. And some melon—"

"And ham, please?" For Federico's stomach, just in case. He sliced the cheese—a sheep's cheese, with a rind—and offered Michelangelo the first piece. Every gesture mattered.

244

"What's the story you wanted to tell?" Michelangelo asked through a forkful of stew.

Federico savored a mouthful of stew. Never in his life had food tasted this good. "I know this girl. She's . . ."

Michelangelo poured himself wine. "She's crazy. She's a girl."

"Not crazy." Federico paused. "She knows things. She knows the future."

"Hmph." Michelangelo sipped at his wine. "Claims she's a prophet, eh?"

Federico picked his words. "Think about five hundred years ago. Do we know anything about that time? I don't. I know Virgil and Latin, but the name of pope in the year 1011? The fashions? The King of France?"

Michelangelo frowned. He shook his head.

"Exactly. Five hundred years from now, we'll be forgotten. The great dukes of Mantua will be a line in a book. Only dust."

Michelangelo sliced into the sausage. "This is a lovely conversation. Where's the bread?"

Federico handed him a loaf. "But that's where this girl comes in. She has seen Rome—the city of Rome—five hundred years hence. She has seen the Sistine Chapel. She has seen your ceiling in its finished glory."

Michelangelo paused. "The ceiling?" He set down the bread. "Finished?"

Federico nodded. "She has seen it in the company of scholars, with travelers from all over the world. Pilgrims from lands farther than China. Countries we don't yet know. All these people desperate to see. All of them, looking up. Gazing at the ceiling. And on the lips of every visitor is one word."

The silence stretched between them. The candles guttered on the table; in the fireplace, an ember popped. The night pressed against the windows as if the darkness listened, too.

"The word, Master—" Federico pushed away his empty bowl. "The word is *Michelangelo*." He wiped off his knife and sheathed it. "Or it would have been." He stood up. "Now they'll never get the chance."

Michelangelo sat like a muscled slab of marble.

Federico strode across the inn. Behind him, Michelangelo was silent. Did he care? Had he even heard? Federico couldn't ask. Every gesture mattered.

He paused at the door. "Goodbye, Master. May you find good fortune in Florence." He shut the door behind him.

"Stable man," he cried loudly, in case Michelangelo was listening. In case the sculptor—the vainest man Federico knew, in a city drowning in vanity—had pride enough to seek immortality. "Stable man! A horse, if you would? I'm returning to Rome."

## Chapter 30
### THE PEACOCK AND THE HANGMAN

Bee lay sobbing on the scaffolding, her heart shattered into a thousand tiny pieces. On the ceiling above her, Adam shuffled out of Eden, his face crumpled in despair. But he didn't hurt as much as Bee. "Moo!" she called. But Moo couldn't hear her. Moo didn't even know Bee was alive.

On the scaffolding below her, Raphael wept, too.

*We're sorry but this number is not in service. . . .* This is what happened when people went back in time. They screwed up the future. How dumb Bee had been.

"Such talent!" Raphael wept. "Such talent, compared to me."

If Bee hadn't gone into the wardrobe, Fred would still

be in Rome instead of panicking the Swiss Guards. He was probably chasing Michelangelo right now.

Was Fred going to die?

"Why should I bother?" Raphael wailed. Easy for him to say.

*At least Fred is doing something,* Bee thought miserably. The realization made her feel even worse. He wasn't just lying around bawling.

She swiped her eyes on her sleeve. She wished she could blow her nose. She should do something, too. Chip in. Not by chasing Michelangelo, duh. But something.

She could get the drawing.

Bee blinked. If she got the drawing, then Miss Bother wouldn't have a blank space over her fireplace. Maybe Miss Bother would be okay. Maybe Moo would study the drawing and meet Mom and they'd have Bee. . . . she didn't know! But something was better than nothing. She had to try.

She sat up. "Excuse me." It sounded more like a croak because of her crying. "Excuse me, Master." She crept down the scaffolding toward him. To the beautiful prophet painted on the wall.

"What is it?" Raphael asked despondently.

Bee crouched beside him. "I'm sorry, but you, um . . . you still need to draw me."

Raphael gave her a withering look. "I have no talent. Don't you see?"

"But you have to." Bee bit her lip, forcing back tears. "You promised. If you don't—" She paused, trying to find the right words. "If you don't, it won't be good."

"I won't be good?" Raphael scoffed, gesturing at the ceiling. "Look at all this! I'm no good at all."

"No, I meant that it won't be good. . . ." Although he was right. A good person would draw her right now. A good person would make sure to be drawn.

"I can't," Raphael declared, turning his back.

Bee sat there. She didn't know what else to do.

Raphael glared at her over his shoulder.

"Please?"

Raphael sighed. "Oh, fine." He flopped open his satchel. "It doesn't matter, anyway."

It probably didn't, Bee agreed. But they had to try.

She watched Raphael tug out his sketchbook and ink, his box of pens. When Bee was little, she'd sit with her box of crayons at Moo's desk as Moo typed. *I'm working, too,* Bee would say as she colored. That was one of the reasons Bee loved Moo's poster of the prophet: the colors. Orange. Green. Blue. Almost like crayons.

A tear slid down her cheek. Poor Fred, she thought. He'd been living without his mother for a year! But at least Fred knew his mother existed. At least he'd be able to go home.

Unless he died.

Raphael bent over the page. His pen scratched.

But what if Raphael's drawing didn't work? What if it wasn't the right one? What if it only helped Miss Bother? Could Bee even live without parents? All these fears swirling in her brain, round and round and round . . .

Her back hurt. She'd been sitting forever, it felt like, in the flickering lantern light.

As she watched, the flame went out. A sunbeam caught the far wall of the chapel. The prophet's orange robe came to life, and her blue headscarf. Her rosy cheeks, as fresh as new paint. Daylight caught her worried eyes. Hazel eyes, like Moo's.

"Are you done?" Bee asked. She wanted Moo so badly.

"Almost . . . Lift your chin, please." Raphael studied his work.

The sunshine brightened. "Because I really want to go home."

"Mmm."

"Is the drawing . . . " She could hardly bear to ask. "Is it good?"

"No." Triumphantly he held out the sketchbook. "It is brilliant."

Bee exhaled a long breath. There it was. The thick lashes, the downturned mouth, the scratch. The mole. "It's me." And so sad! "It's fantastic."

"I know." Raphael shot a look at the ceiling. "The best art in the world?" he snorted. "Ha."

Something was missing, though. "You need to sign it."

"Of course." He dipped his pen. "There." He handed it to Bee. "Keep the book if you'd like."

"Really?" Bee clutched the sketchbook to her chest.

"I have many." Smoothly he packed his supplies into the satchel. "Shall we?" He eased onto the ladder, lantern over his arm. "Such a peculiar sense of color," he murmured as he descended, gazing at the ceiling.

Bee followed, sketchbook in her teeth. She would never, ever let it go.

Raphael chuckled as he climbed down. "Do you know what Leonardo da Vinci calls Michelangelo? The baker. Because he is always covered in dust. Marble dust, to be sure, not flour. But still, it's amusing."

Bee reached the bottom. She needed to get to the wardrobe!

Raphael sauntered across the floor, still gazing up. "Plus he has no sense of massing. . . ." He waved Bee through the door, and locked it, and handed her the key. "Sir Federico's, I believe?"

"Thank you," Bee said, distracted. Which way to the corridor? Through that arch?

"What a marvelous experience." Raphael fell in beside her, his arm around her shoulders. "Though I'm sure I can paint better." A group of men in work clothes passed, Raphael greeting them by name. He gave Bee an affectionate shake. "Do you know what we in the studio call Michelangelo? The hangman—because he dresses in black and is always alone. Ah, genius. How it torments us."

Numbly Bee nodded, clutching the sketchbook and key.

They reached the construction, the rooms already crowded with painters. "Giulio!" Raphael cried, at last letting go of Bee. "I have the most splendid idea for a figure. What do you think of this pose?"

There: the door to the corridor. Bee ran for it, before Raphael could grab her again, or that Swiss Guard, or anyone in the year 1511. She needed home! She tugged the door open, zooming for the wardrobe.

What if the wardrobe didn't work? *Don't think that—*

Somewhere in the distance, a door slammed. "Bee?" Racing footsteps.

"Fred?" Even with her worries, Bee burst into a smile. *Fred!*

"Bee!" He pounded up the corridor into view. Wow, was he dirty. Dust caked his face; brown stained his sleeve—

"Is that blood?" Bee gasped. And: "You're alive!"

"I'm so glad you're here!" Fred threw his arms wide, laughing with joy. "I've been riding for hours with Michelangelo. All he did was complain about money."

"He's alive, too?" Bee spun Fred in a bear hug. "And look—" She thrust out the sketchbook, flipping it open. "Look at this."

"Oh!" Fred breathed. "He did it."

Bee pressed the book into his hands. "And he signed it! *Raphael.* I watched." What a day. The sky hung above them like a rich blue bowl; the sun shone with the pure white of morning. Doves cooed in the trees. She tucked the Sistine key into Fred's knife sheath. "That's for you."

Fred couldn't take his eyes from the drawing. "It's so beautiful. Will it be enough, do you think, for Miss Bother?"

"I think." Bee's smile faded. "Um . . ." She swallowed. "How do we get it to her?"

"You hand it over, like this." He demonstrated. "It requires a certain action of the forearms, but with practice it is not difficult."

"Ha ha. I mean how does it end up in Miss Bother's house? I can't just carry it through the wardrobe, can I?" The blank spot above the fireplace would still be there when she went back.

"Hmm." Fred frowned. "'Erbert found it in Mantua, he told me. In a trunk."

They walked together, brooding on this. They were almost at the wardrobe.

"So Herbert went to Mantua," Bee sighed. "And he found a trunk with a drawing in it. You know, like people do."

"And rebuilt the trunk into the closet." Ignoring her sarcasm.

"The wardrobe," Bee corrected. It was right there in front of them. She so wanted to go through! But she couldn't. Not until they figured this out.

Fred sank onto the stack of planks. "This whole thing makes me dizzy." He held up the sketchbook with its drawing of Bee. "What am I supposed to do? Take this to Mantua?"

"Maybe." Bee shrugged helplessly. "You make a trunk and, you know, you put it in."

"And hope 'Erbert finds it in four hundred years?"

"I guess. You're the boss of Mantua, right?"

Fred looked at her. He nodded. He set the sketchbook under his arm, and straightened his shoulders, and raised his chin. He looked like a warrior, kind of. "Then I shall. I shall make it so. And in the meantime you may bring me peanuts."

"Very funny." Oh. He wasn't joking. "You're not joking."

"About peanuts? Never." Fred stood. He opened the wardrobe with a bow. "My lady?"

"Why, thank you." Bee bowed back. Not a bad bow, she thought. "See you at midnight?"

"Naturally." Fred smiled.

Bee paused at the wardrobe door, snapping her fingers. "Wait—wasn't there something else you needed? Some kind of animal? A goat, maybe?"

Fred's smile widened. "I think you know." He held the sketchbook close. "And chocolate, please. Don't forget."

"I won't," said Bee. "See you soon." She stepped through.

## Chapter 31

## A BEGINNING AND AN END

The closet door shut with a click.

Federico eased it open, just to check. Empty, naturally. "Till midnight." How many hours until Juno and chocolate and Bee! He missed them already. Yawning, he gave the sketchbook a pat. How nice it felt to help Miss Bother, five hundred years away. He'd need a trunk to get this drawing to Herbert; that was a puzzle. At the moment, however, he most needed sleep—

The palace door crashed open, and His Holiness marched in. "Spies?" he roared over his shoulder.

Bramante scurried after him, trailed by workmen. "Your Holiness, I can explain—"

The pope spun toward Bramante, purple with rage. "You installed a machine built for spies in our palace?"

Bramante smiled weakly, glancing at the closet. "But it did not work." Anxiously he jangled his keys. "Even my dear friend Leonardo said as much. . . ." He beckoned to the workmen. "Come, men. Destroy this contraption, for His Holiness and the goodness of Rome."

"No!" Federico leaped forward. "You can't! You must not!"

"And burn it," Bramante added, his eyes on the pope.

"Please." Federico threw himself in front of the closet. "Please, Your Holiness. It's special to me." He fell to his knees, tugging at the pope. "I'll take it, I'll keep it, I'll make sure there's no danger. I beg you."

The pope flicked back his robes. He would not look at Federico. "We won't tolerate spies."

"Precisely," Bramante declared. "Destroy it, men."

"No!" wailed Federico—too late, for already the workmen had ripped off the door. "No!"

"He sounds like a child," the pope said with distaste, backing away. "We don't like children." Hastily he retreated to the palace. "This caterwauling makes us quite ill. We must have lunch soon, to settle our stomach. . . ." He squeezed his way through the door.

Piece by piece, the workmen broke up the closet.

Federico watched, too filled with grief even to breathe.

"I had no choice." Bramante did his best to sound innocent. "'Twas my neck on the block—"

Again the palace door slammed open. Michelangelo stomped down the corridor. "Ho there, toad!"

"Finish the job," Bramante ordered, ignoring this bellow.

Federico grabbed Michelangelo's arm. "Please, Master! You must stop them."

Michelangelo shrugged him away. "The peacock was in my scaffolding," he announced. "I can smell him!"

"Come, men." Bramante clapped. "Now gather the pieces for the fire."

Numbly Federico stared at the boards. It might as well have been his heart on the floor.

"Did you let him in, toad?" Michelangelo snarled. "Did you give him your key?"

The key.

Federico slipped his hand to his belt. The key.

He set his hand around the cold metal and pulled the key

from his knife sheath. Not far. Only enough for Bramante to see.

Bramante slapped his hand to his key ring. Blood drained from his face as he stared at Michelangelo's fists.

"What's wrong with you, toad?" Michelangelo thundered.

"N-nothing." Bramante tried to swallow.

Federico smiled sweetly—his angel smile, his mother called it. Sometimes it worked even on her. "Master Bramante? Please don't burn this closet."

"You're right—there's no need—" Bramante flapped at the workmen. "We're done here. How l-late it is. Off we go." He herded them toward the palace, mopping his brow.

Michelangelo peered around the empty corridor. "Something just happened."

Federico stared at the strewn scraps of wood. "Master?" he asked. "Can you build a closet?"

"A closet?" Michelangelo scoffed. He marched to the niche in the wall. "I'm an artist—the greatest in the world! They speak of me in China. I don't build closets." Shaking his head, he unlocked the low door to his studio. "I know that peacock was snooping. I'll prove it somehow." He gave Federico a last frustrated glare and was gone.

Alone in the corridor, Federico sagged to the floor. How would he ever see Juno again? Or Bee? His only two friends in the world. His true family. A gentleman should not sob, he knew. But at this moment he was only a boy. A heartbroken, friendless boy.

Footsteps approached. Heavy, but with a light tread. "My lord." A voice as deep as the sea.

Federico wiped his eyes. With effort, he looked up.

The Swiss Guard towered over him. "I am glad to find you at last."

Federico wiped his cheeks. "You found me? Were you looking?"

"Yes. Your governess was quite upset." The Swiss Guard leaned on his sword. "She thought you'd died in a duel or were kidnapped by pirates. Many words came out of her mouth."

A smile found its way to Federico's lips. "Celeste? That's a good way to describe her."

The guard squatted beside Federico, eying the jumble of lumber. "What is this?"

"It used to be a closet." Federico's voice broke. "Now I don't know what it is."

"What would you like it to be?" The guard lifted a board in his huge hands. He closed one eye to look down its edge. "I'm a carpenter, you know."

Federico stared at him. "A carpenter?"

The guard gestured at his uniform. "This pays better. But yes, that's my trade."

"You make things out of wood?"

"That is, I believe, the definition of carpentry."

Like a shaft of sunlight breaking through the clouds, an idea seeped into Federico's head. He gulped. "Could you make this wood into a box, say? A trunk?"

The guard shrugged one massive shoulder. "I could build a trunk when I was younger than you. Is that all you need? Not a fancy lock? A secret compartment?"

Federico straightened. "A secret compartment? You can do that?"

"I am Swiss."

Slowly Federico held out the sketchbook. "Raphael gave me this. Could you hide it?"

The guard nodded his great head. "The work of a moment."

Federico sat back on his heels. "I'm sorry, but I don't know your name. I'm Federico Gonzaga."

The guard took Federico's hand in one massive paw. "Pleased to meet you. I am Franz Giovanni—"

Beside them, the wood shifted. Federico jumped in surprise. Even Franz jumped.

Faintly, as if from far away, came a plaintive cry: "Mrow."

"Juno!" Federico scrabbled at the pile. "Help me, please."

Franz leaned over, scooping up boards. A cat emerged—a lion-colored cat with amber eyes. "Mrow," she complained, her tail lashing.

"Juno!" Federico grabbed her in a great spinning hug.

Franz frowned, his arms full of wood. "Where did she come from?"

"This is Juno," Federico explained, scratching her neck. Graciously Juno accepted, though she kept one eye on the guard. "Juno, this is Franz."

"Mrow." She sounded pleased. Pleased enough.

"And what is this?" Franz peered at a slim box on the floor.

"Chocolate!" Federico set down Juno to snatch up the box. "Take some, please."

Doubtfully Franz tasted it. "We do not have this in Switzerland."

"You should." Federico popped one into his mouth. "They're quite delicious."

"Remarkable," the guard observed, savoring his piece. "You know, my lord, you seem to have a fair number of adventures."

Federico nodded. He did.

"Your page said it was a long story. I should like to hear it someday."

"My page? Oh, you mean Bee. She—he—had to return to his own country." He gulped. "I thought he could come back, but now. . . ." He busied himself gathering the small mirrors that littered the floor, tucking them into his jerkin. It was easier than trying to speak.

"I am sorry, young lord," the guard said gravely. "It is hard to lose friends." He set an armful of lumber against the wall, a neat stack next to the planks.

Juno trotted down the corridor toward the villa. "Mrow," she called over her shoulder.

"She has the correct idea," Franz observed, still gathering boards. "You should return to your rooms before Celeste makes more words."

Carefully, slowly, Federico collected the glass balls and the water-filled globe. He had Juno, yes, and these bits of glass, miraculously intact. But he could not bear the thought of the villa, or Celeste, or the emptiness of the life before him. "Might you escort me?" A few moments of companionship before loneliness drowned him.

Franz arranged the last of the closet on his tidy stack. "'Twould be my pleasure."

Off they set, Juno leading the way. Franz cleared his throat. "You raise an interesting subject, my lord." He gestured to Federico's bloodied sleeve. "I believe you might be in need of a bodyguard."

"A bodyguard?" Federico did not know what to make of this. "Do you know one?"

"I might. I know a carpenter whose time as Swiss Guard soon comes to an end."

"I should talk to him, then." Federico took care to keep his face smooth. But his heart tumbled like a jester. Could this wonderful man be offering to work for him? As Bee would say: Wow.

*I still have Bee,* he realized with a happy smile. He had her in his soul.

"I believe I could arrange a meeting between you and this

Swiss Guard who is also a carpenter." Franz's arm swung next to Federico.

"I would like that." Casually, as if it were no matter, Federico took the guard's hand—a massive hand, calloused from a lifetime of toil. A rush of happiness filled him. Never in his life had he felt safer.

"How is the girl, by the way?"

"Miss Bother, you mean?" Federico reflected on Bee. On Herbert, who cared. He looked down at the box of chocolates, hidden in the closet just for him. Life, it seemed, had worked out for Miss Bother. He smiled. "We saved her, I think."

## Chapter 32

## THE AUCTION

Bee stepped out of the wardrobe. "Juno?" she whispered.

Silence in Herbert's office. No *mrow.* No padding of paws. No red fingernails breaking in. Just the wardrobe and the desk and the dull ceiling light.

She took another step. Dust still covered the desk—dust and dead flies. The encyclopedia. The phone. Note cards with NO TIME PASSES and HOW DOES THE CAT MOVE? The calendar. An old-fashioned engraving of a guy in a puffy coat with a dog—

Wait. The picture hadn't been there last time. Bee squinted at the caption. A lot of cursive writing. The word *TITIAN.*

Who was Titian?

A sound drifted through the bookcase. She spun. "Juno?" she called.

With a deep breath, she eased the bookcase open. The woman with the clipboard wasn't there anymore! The woman or the man.

Bee slumped, so relieved that for a moment she barely could stand.

But wait—the bookcase wasn't dusty. It had been dusty before. Now, though, the shelves were clean, and the floor. And those noises! The clink of glasses. Murmuring.

Bee squeezed her eyes shut. She'd been so close. What was she going to do now?

"Bee?"

Her head came up.

"Beatrice Rosetti Bliss, dov'è la mia amora?" *Where is my love?*

"Moo!" Bee hurled herself down the stairs. Moo! Right there by the bedroom with her curly black hair and huge smile, a little box in her hands.

"Cosa fai, Bombo?" *What are you doing, Bumblebee?* "You've been up here a while."

Bee threw herself into Moo's arms. "You're here!"

"You think I'd miss Nana?" She rumpled Bee's hair. "Attento, how'd you get dirty?"

"You're here." Bee squeezed her, breathing in the smell of soap and books and Moo-ness. Moo was back. Moo, who knew everything— "Hey, who's Titian?"

Moo laughed. "He was an artist in the 1500s. Anyone important, he painted them."

"Wait—he's an artist?" Bee had thought it was a picture *of* Titian.

"Sì." Moo plucked at Bee's jerkin. "What is this?"

Bee caught sight of the box. "Wait, is that—?"

"To celebrate. What's the face? It's like you've never seen candy before."

"Thank you! Wait here, okay?" Bee leaped up the stairs, past the bookcase, and put the box on the wardrobe floor. Chocolate peanuts. "Enjoy," she whispered. She'd explain it to Fred later.

She leaned over the desk, studying the guy with the puffy coat. *An engraving of Duke Federico II Gonzaga of Mantua,* it said in cursive. *From the original portrait by TITIAN.*

"Fred," she whispered, hand to her mouth. He was a grown-up now, with a beard. He had a coat with lots of embroidery, and rings on his fingers, and a little white dog. His eyes twinkled.

"Bombo?" Moo called. "Where have you gone to?"

"I'm here!" She dashed back down the stairs.

"What is wrong?" Moo wiped Bee's cheek. "Are you crying?"

"Nothing." She stiffened—there was that sound again. Like *oooh*, kind of. "What's that?"

Moo chuckled, hugging Bee as they went down the stairs. "You're so funny." She ran her fingers over Bee's collar. "Bombo? This is hand-stitched."

"Oh, no," Bee moaned. The house was clean! And there were people here, too. A whole crowd in the front hall in fancy clothes. And—

"Mom!" Bee leaped down the last step to hug her. "I love you I love you I love you—"

"I love you, too, Queen Bee." Mom laughed. "Now hush."

And the dining room! Now it had white curtains and freshly painted walls. Twenty people stood staring at the table, at a cell phone. A man in a bow tie gave Bee a shocked look.

Mom grinned at him, hugging Bee. "Isn't the resemblance amazing?"

He nodded, gaping at Bee, and slowly turned back to the

phone. ". . . from Dubai," a British voice was saying. "That takes the bidding to four point eight."

Mom gave Bee a squeeze. "I can't believe you wandered off. You almost missed it."

A woman in a blue dress stared at Bee. "You're right," she told Mom. "It's quite a resemblance."

The man beside her shook his head. "It's like Raphael actually saw her. How does it feel to be headed for a museum?" he asked Bee.

What was going on?

"May I remind the audience"—the cell phone again—"that this is the first signed Raphael drawing in many years. . . ."

Bee glanced at the wall above the fireplace. It was empty. She gulped.

Something had hung there, though, once. A nail still stuck out from the wall. A light shone down from the ceiling. An old lady stood in front of the fireplace—a really old lady with a cane. She wore a nubby skirt with a matching pink jacket, the kind of outfit Fred would love.

"Please hold your applause," the cell phone said.

The old lady had lipstick on, and shiny black shoes with pink bows.

"And from the Metropolitan Museum of Art," said the cell phone, "a bid of five million dollars." Everyone in the dining room gasped. The man in the bow tie covered his face.

A noise from the kitchen: "Mrow!"

All around Bee, people jumped. But not her. She knew Juno by now. "Hey there." Bee smiled. "Welcome back." Juno must have come in through the cat door.

Juno curled round Bee's legs, blinking up at her with black-lined eyes. Her tail drew smiles in the air. "Mrow," she answered. *Good to see you again.*

"What's that cat doing here?" the bow tie man hissed. "I'm allergic!"

The old lady put a hand on his arm. Her skin was so thin that blue veins showed through. "Don't worry. She belongs here."

"Mrow," Juno agreed, ambling up the stairs. Bee turned to watch her.

"How do you know that cat?" Mom asked, her arm around Bee.

"I just do." Bee grinned. "How does the cat move," she whispered to herself. Juno knew where she was going.

". . . and the Getty Museum has raised the bidding to six."

"Mrow," Juno announced from the landing. *Goodbye.*

The old lady leaned over her cane, trying to see. "Goodbye, Juno," she called.

Moo smoothed Bee's jerkin. "Seriously, Bombo. Where did you find this?"

"Long story. Is that really Miss Bother?"

Mom chuckled. "You still call Nana by that name after all these years?"

The old lady looked at Bee. Her eyes drifted down Bee's dirty white shirt—an old-fashioned shirt. Bee's belt with its little knife sheath. Her quilted gray jerkin. Her hose with their built-in shoes. "Beatrice," the old lady whispered. Bee could hear her even through the crowd.

The cell phone voice rose. "Going once, going twice. . . ."

Suddenly Bee's eyes were filled with tears.

Mom held her tight. "You okay?"

Moo leaned over. "Are you in trouble?"

"I was." Bee wiped her eyes. "But I fixed it."

The old lady raised a teacup, toasting Bee like it was just the two of them in the house. "Grazie," she whispered. *Thank you.*

". . . and sold!" the cell phone cried.

"Sold?" Mom cried. "It sold?" She threw her arms around Moo. Moo was screaming. The woman in the blue dress hugged the man beside her, cheering like crazy. The people in the dining room shrieked. The man in the bow tie blew his nose.

Miss Bother didn't move, though. Nana. She just kept watching Bee. "You made everything better, Beatrice," she whispered. Their secret. "You made everything good."

# AUTHOR'S NOTE

Federico II Gonzaga was a real kid, born in the year 1500 in tiny Mantua—now part of Italy—in a castle with five hundred rooms. Beginning in 1510, he spent three years in Rome as a hostage of Pope Julius II. The two became friends, the boy even nursing the old man through malaria. Federico's mother, Isabella d'Este, one of the great art collectors in Europe, wrote Federico and his tutors countless bossy letters. Following the pope's death in 1513, Federico returned to Mantua, becoming duke in 1520.

Raphael's portrait of Federico can still be seen in *The School of Athens,* the curly-haired boy on the left. (There is controversy over whether this boy is in fact Federico, but I'm certain of it.) The painter Raphael was handsome, charming, and witty, with a constant circle of students and admirers. Everyone loved him . . . except Michelangelo. The two trash-talked each other whenever they met, Raphael usually winning. He actually called Michelangelo a hangman. Legend has it that Raphael borrowed a key to the Sistine Chapel from the architect Bramante and snuck in to study the ceiling by torchlight. To the best of my knowledge he did not sketch Bee, but a quick internet search of "Raphael drawings" will show his incredible talent.

As you've probably gathered, Michelangelo had issues. He changed his clothes so infrequently that when he took off his boots, "the skin came away like a snake"—that's how one friend described it. He fought nonstop with Julius II and once got so angry that he threw a board at the pope from the top of the scaffolding. He then panicked and fled Rome on horse-back at midnight, chased by the pope's spies. Michelangelo didn't seem to mind young Federico, however. He even let the boy give tours of the Sistine Chapel while he worked.

Amazingly enough, the great artist and inventor Leonardo da Vinci lived in Mantua before Federico was born and drew a portrait of Isabella d'Este. By 1511, however, he had fled Italy's endless wars for France, where he worked for the king and sketched cats. Perhaps he invented a time machine, but since many of his notebooks have been lost, we'll never know for sure. He called Michelangelo a baker, as an insult.

Italians did indeed eat spaghetti with cinnamon sugar because tomatoes weren't yet known in Europe; like chocolate and peanuts, they're from the New World. And for a time canaries were so popular that they were worth their weight in gold.